"Kelly, there's no such thing as true love..."

She turned away so that he wouldn't see her hurt. "I think it exists. I don't want to settle for less. Now, if you'll excuse me, I've got a lot to do. Good night, Mike." She held the door open.

The sight of him walking away, then the sound of the front door closing, were just about the loneliest things Kelly could imagine. Mike Cameron had just asked her to marry him, and he was serious. Not only that, he was angry that she'd refused his proposal.

She was pregnant. She was unemployed. She was moving. She was probably crazy. What woman in her right mind would say no to a handsome hunk like Mike? She reminded herself that she was doing this to protect him.

But if she was doing the right thing, why did it feel so wrong and awful?

Dear Reader,

Happy Valentine's Day! Silhouette Romance's Valentine to you is our special lineup this month, starting with *Daddy by Decision* by bestselling, award-winning author Lindsay Longford. When rugged cowboy Buck Riley sees his estranged ex with a child who looks just like him, he believes the little boy is his son. True or not, that belief in his heart—and his love for mother and child—is all he needs to be a FABULOUS FATHER.

And we're celebrating love and marriage with I'M YOUR GROOM, a five-book promotion about five irresistible heroes who say "I do" for a lifetime of love. In Carolyn Zane's *It's Raining Grooms,* a preacher's daughter prays for a husband and suddenly finds herself engaged to her gorgeous childhood nemesis. *To Wed Again?* by DeAnna Talcott tells the story of a divorced couple who are blessed with a second chance at marriage when they become instant parents. Next, in Judith Janeway's *An Accidental Marriage,* the maid of honor and the best man are forced to act like the eloped newlyweds when the bride's parents arrive!

Plus, two authors sure to become favorites make their Romance debuts this month. In *Husband Next Door* by Anne Ha, a very confirmed bachelor is reformed into marriage material, and in *Wedding Rings and Baby Things* by Teresa Southwick, an any-minute mom-to-be says "I do" to a marriage of convenience that leads to a lifetime of love....

I hope you enjoy all six of these wonderful books.

Warm wishes,

Melissa Senate,
Senior Editor
Silhouette Books

Please address questions and book requests to:
Silhouette Reader Service
U.S.: 3010 Walden Ave., P.O. Box 1325, Buffalo, NY 14269
Canadian: P.O. Box 609, Fort Erie, Ont. L2A 5X3

WEDDING RINGS AND BABY THINGS

Teresa Southwick

Silhouette

ROMANCE™

Published by Silhouette Books

America's Publisher of Contemporary Romance

To Jim, my big brother and very own legal eagle.
Thanks for giving me the words to make Mike a hero.
For always being there and understanding, you have
my everlasting gratitude.

 SILHOUETTE BOOKS

ISBN 0-373-19209-6

WEDDING RINGS AND BABY THINGS

Copyright © 1997 by Teresa Ann Southwick

Printed in U.S.A.

TERESA SOUTHWICK

is a native Californian with ties to each coast, since she was conceived in the East and born in the West. Living with her husband of twenty-five years and two handsome sons, she is surrounded by heroes. Reading has been her passion since she was a girl. She couldn't be more delighted that her dream of writing full-time has come true. Her favorite things include: holding a baby, the fragrance of jasmine, walks on the beach, the patter of rain on the roof, and above all—happy endings.

Teresa also writes historical romance novels under the same name.

*Kelly Walker and Mike Cameron
request the honor of your presence at their marriage
of convenience on Saturday evening. The ceremony
will take place at the groom's residence on
Peachland Avenue, Newhall, California,
with a reception immediately following the exchange
of vows. Apologies are hereby extended for the
short notice, although there is a story behind it—
one you'll see but not hear for three more months.
Please join Mike and Kelly as they begin
their life together in friendship,
perhaps to fall in love....*

Chapter One

She'd picked a bad time to swear off men.

Not that it was a permanent situation, Kelly Walker amended. Besides, her condition wasn't exactly conducive to getting involved with men, and that was the way she wanted to keep it.

On the other hand, her condition was probably the reason she had been summoned to the administration office in the high school where she taught. She stared at the wavy, light-and-dark wood grain in the door marked Principal. As much as she tried to tell herself differently, it wasn't likely that Mr. Bloomhurst had summoned her here to discuss her interpretation of *Hamlet.* He probably wanted to talk about the fact that she was six months pregnant, not married—and not getting married.

Stevenson High School was located in Newhall, the small California town where she'd grown up. No one knew better than she how people talked, how quickly gossip circulated. She had expected when this news got out it would spread like soft butter on a hot muffin.

Since she hadn't begun to really show until the last week or so, she had been able to keep her condition quiet. Only two people were supposed to know that she was going to have a baby. Susan Wishart, who taught in the classroom next to Kelly's, and Mike Cameron, head of the math department, head football coach and her very best friend in the world. She had made them promise not to say anything until she could break the news to Mr. Bloomhurst herself. As many times as she'd rehearsed everything in her mind, she still wasn't prepared for this chat with her boss.

She had figured on telling him at the end of the school year when the next term assignments were given out. It was now the beginning of May. In the Arizona school where she'd taught before, teachers didn't find out until the last week before summer vacation what they would be teaching in the fall. She was just finishing up her second year at Stevenson and was still getting used to how things were done here.

She had thought she'd been able to camouflage her swelling body with loose clothes, but she had been getting some long, curious looks. First the eyebrows went up when someone's eyes dropped to her midsection. Then the gaze lifted to see if her face had gotten rounder. Then the examination dropped below her belly to her legs to determine if she had put on weight everywhere. After all of this, which took about a second and a half, the person pretended she hadn't noticed a thing. So far everyone who was perceptive enough to give her the ritual once-over hadn't said anything.

Everyone, that is, except Elizabeth McCutcheon. Earlier today, she had asked Kelly point-blank if she was going to have a baby. Kelly had said yes. Mrs. McCutcheon hadn't let it drop there. She said she hadn't heard that Kelly had gotten married. Kelly told her she hadn't. Even in this small town, the majority of people wouldn't have pushed the issue, but Mrs. McCutcheon happened to be the president of the district's Parent Advisory Committee.

Hence Kelly's summons to Mr. Bloomhurst after school.

She took a deep breath and knocked.

"Come in," a voice called out.

She opened the door and walked inside.

Cliff Bloomhurst glanced up from the paperwork on his desk. "Hi, Kelly."

"Mr. Bloomhurst."

He smiled, looking at her over the half glasses he needed only for reading and now had balanced on the tip of his nose. The sleeves of his white shirt were rolled up to the elbow, and his red-and-blue-striped tie was loosened just enough to release the button at his neck. His thinning brown hair was peppered with gray and there was genuine warmth in his light blue eyes. She liked him a lot. He was a nice man.

"Come on in. And shut the door, please." His voice was a sort of down-home drawl that normally put her completely at ease. But not today.

Kelly did as he asked, then perched on the edge of one of the green plastic chairs in front of his desk. Nervously she rested her elbows on the metal armrests and laced her fingers together.

"I know what this is about," she said. "Let's cut to the chase. I'm going to have a baby."

"So I heard."

"I planned to tell you soon. The baby is due at the

end of July or the beginning of August. I will be here on the first day of school in September.''

''I wish I didn't have to ask, but…are you planning to marry the baby's father?''

''No.''

Even if Doug Hammond had proposed instead of telling her not to expect any support, she wouldn't tie herself to a man who was so underhanded and untrustworthy. She was sorry she hadn't seen sooner what a jerk Doug was. After that conversation, she hadn't expected to hear from him again. But in the last couple weeks, he had left messages on her answering machine. She hadn't returned them and hoped he would get the hint that she wanted him out of her life forever. She couldn't stand the sight of the man, but she would never be sorry about the baby she now carried.

Mr. Bloomhurst looked genuinely sympathetic. ''Then my hands are tied, Kelly. Liz McCutcheon went to the school board after she spoke to you today. They called me with a decision. You won't be back in September.''

Kelly's heart sank. ''I don't understand.''

''You're a fine teacher. No one knows that or appreciates the job you do more than me. But the school board won't permit a pregnant, unmarried teacher in the classroom. They're concerned about the example it sets for the students.''

''But this is the nineties, Mr. Bloomhurst.''

He nodded grimly. ''I know. But this is Newhall, California, Small Town, U.S.A. It's a nice place to live. But that can be a double-edged sword.''

''I won't be pregnant in September.''

''Are you planning to keep the child?''

"Of course!" Kelly was shocked that he would even ask. It would never occur to her to give away her child.

"You won't be married, either, and you'll still have a child out of wedlock. I did my best to change their minds, but they were adamant."

Kelly was numb. She knew that was a good thing. She didn't want to go hysterical in front of this man. "I suppose there's nothing I can do?"

He shook his head. "If you had tenure, you could probably fight the ruling."

She stood up and gripped the back of the chair so tightly her knuckles turned white. "Do you want me to finish out the last four weeks?"

"I'd appreciate it."

"But I'm still pregnant. What about Mrs. Mc-Cutcheon?"

"I'll handle Liz." He looked down for a moment, then back up at her. "I know this is hypocritical, but I'd like to keep the news quiet and have you finish up with your classes until the end of the year. It would be disruptive to the students to bring in a substitute now."

She nodded. "I wouldn't do anything to hurt the kids. Some of them need these grades for college."

"I appreciate that, Kelly." He folded his hands and looked at her a little uncomfortably. "May I ask you a personal question? You don't have to answer if you don't want to."

"I have nothing to hide."

"There's a rumor…" He cleared his throat. "Is Mike the baby's father?"

"No!" Mike Cameron? The idea shocked her. Then she almost laughed out loud. She'd known Mike since she was a kid. Once she'd had a crush on him, but she'd gotten over that years ago. "We're good friends, nothing more. I rent his guest house—" Aha, that was probably why someone, probably Mrs. Busybody Mc-Cutcheon, had jumped to some wild conclusions.

"I'm sorry. I had to ask. It was a stupid question. If he was the father we wouldn't be having this discussion." Mr. Bloomhurst took off his glasses. He stood up and held out his hand. "If there's anything I can ever do, just let me know."

"I will," Kelly said, putting her fingers in his palm. She knew he truly meant what he said, but she couldn't help being angry and upset. As nice as he was, he was still a man. As much as she needed one right now, *a.* he was already married, and *b.* she had sworn off men…maybe forever.

Kelly drove into Mike's driveway, past his large Spanish-style home, then braked in front of the smaller guest house. She leaned to the left and pulled the lever to pop the trunk on her four-door car before getting out to remove the empty cardboard boxes. As she moved purposefully up the curved, brick walkway to her front porch, she tried to shake the fear she was feeling about finding a new job and a place to live.

After unlocking the heavy oak door, she clicked on the front porch light and tossed the boxes inside, then retrieved the rest from the car. When she was finished, she slung her purse on the parsons bench just beside the door of her two-bedroom apartment. With the flick of a switch on the wall, brass lamps illuminated the interior of her comfortable living room with the floral sofa and matching love seat. Oak tables sat on either end of the sofa with a coffee table in front. Her low-heeled shoes sank in the thick hunter green carpet. All the emotions she had been fending off all day gathered into a lump in her throat. How she was going to miss this place.

She recalled when Mike had insisted that her mother pick out the color of the rug, just before they'd moved in. Ill as she was, Margaret Walker had perked up visibly at the excitement of redecorating. Kelly would always be grateful for Mike's kindness to her mother.

That's why she had to protect him now.

It was evening, after seven. She hadn't eaten, but she wasn't hungry. She had spent the time since leaving Mr. Bloomhurst making decisions about what to do. The first one was to move.

After kicking off her shoes, she took a box into the kitchen and started removing things that she hardly ever used from the topmost shelves of her cupboards.

The clatter she made nearly drowned out the doorbell, and she wasn't sure she'd actually heard it. But a second later an insistent ringing told her loud and clear that pregnancy had not affected her ears.

In her bare feet she padded to the front door and opened it.

"Where the hell have you been?" Mike Cameron glared at her and barged through the doorway.

"Hi, Mike. I'm fine, thanks. How are you? Come on in," she said, closing the door. Turning her back on him, she headed through the dining room back to the kitchen. She squatted down and started putting dish towels and odds and ends into a box.

Mike was hot on her heels. She heard his athletic shoes squeak on the tile floor as he stopped short behind her. "I was worried. When you didn't show up to tutor Jake, I was about to call the cops."

Kelly groaned and stood up. "I'm sorry, Mike. I completely forgot."

"What's wrong?" he asked. His dark, almost black, eyes bored into her as if he could see every single secret she had.

"What makes you think there's something wrong?"

"Because you're the most responsible, organized, punctual person I know."

"Watch it. You'll turn my head with flattery like that."

"Cut it out, Kelly. What's going on? Where were you? It's not like you to forget about one of your students."

"I had a bad day. I'll call Jake right now and see if he's available."

She started for the phone, which was right next to where Mike stood in the doorway. When she caught a glimpse of his face, she stopped. Every once in a while she was taken aback by his athletic good looks. His dark hair was cut short, and more often than not he wore a baseball cap that said Stevenson Football on it. He was thirty-five years old, but still boyish looking in spite of the shadow of beard that darkened his jaw. She studied him critically and realized he appeared boyish only when he was smiling, which he was definitely not doing now. At the moment he glowered at her, and his eyes smoldered with anger.

That surprised her. She felt badly that she had missed her appointment, but she had a sneaking suspicion Jake Saterfield was relieved that she hadn't shown up. Mike's star running back put English composition in the same category that the average person put a root canal.

Mike seemed to fill the doorway of her kitchen. "Don't bother calling him. He went to his girlfriend's house to study."

"Jessica is an honors student. If they actually get some work done, he'll do fine on his test in Susan's class tomorrow."

"The hell with his test tomorrow."

"I thought you were concerned about his grade and his eligibility to play in September."

"I am. But right now I'm more concerned about you. I asked you where you were. Hey, what are you doing with these boxes?"

"I'm packing."

"I can see that. Why are you packing? You shouldn't be doing that kind of stuff. You're pregnant, for God's sake." He crossed his arms over his chest and she couldn't help noticing how his red T-shirt pulled tight around his powerful bicep. He was in tip-top physical shape, and reminded Kelly just how ungainly she looked right now. His black shorts showed off his athletic build, right down to his narrow waist and muscular, well-formed thighs. Mike was enough to make a woman's heart beat double-time. If that woman hadn't sworn off men, of course.

Kelly had always thought Mike was a hunk in stretch cotton, since the very first time she'd seen him when her older brother Jim had brought him home after football practice. But there had never been anything of a romantic nature in her relationship with Mike. He had always treated her like a younger sister, and that had killed her crush pretty quickly. But that didn't mean she was deaf, dumb and blind. He was a good-looking man, too sexy for his own good, a fact proven by a string of broken female hearts over the years.

"Since when has pregnancy been a debilitating disease?" she asked snappishly.

Mike's eyebrows lifted at her tone, even though she

hadn't meant to be sharp. Without a word, he walked over to her and gently held her upper arms, squeezing them reassuringly. As he scanned her face, concern replaced irritation.

"Kelly, something's happened. Tell me what's wrong."

She fixed her gaze on the tab collar of his shirt, dismayed that she felt very close to tears. That hadn't happened to her since getting the news. Why now, in front of Mike?

"I've been fired."

He frowned. "Fired?"

"Yes, as in canned, sacked and let go. As of the end of the school year."

"But you're one of the best teachers Cliff has. I don't understand."

"Don't blame Mr. Bloomhurst. He didn't want to do it. The school board made the decision. It's because of the baby," she said, placing one hand protectively on her abdomen. "Actually, that's not entirely true. It's because I'm not married to the baby's father."

"Any woman who marries that jerk should have her head examined."

"Don't start, Mike, or I'll be forced to bring up Bambi."

"Her name was not Bambi. It was Jennifer."

"Same thing," Kelly said. Suddenly she was exhausted. "I'm going to sit down. If you can be supportive and appropriately sympathetic, you're welcome to join me in the living room. If not, go away."

"Come on," he said, taking her hand and leading her to the sofa in front of the red brick fireplace.

Mike sat down beside her. He had been relieved when he heard Kelly's car come up the drive and saw the lights go on in the guest house. As far as he knew, she hadn't missed an appointment for anything since he and her brother, Jim, had kidnapped her for breakfast on her eighteenth birthday and she hadn't shown up to get her hair cut.

Mike half turned so he could see Kelly's face, just as she tucked a dark strand of hair behind her ear. Over the years, he'd seen her with long and short styles, but he decided he liked this sophisticated, page boy look best. Her thick mahogany hair hit her just about chin length and drew his attention to her face. Purple smudges darkened her skin, just below her green eyes. She looked delicate and fragile. He hated that she was losing her job, because she was a fine teacher, and she had a lot to offer her students. Mostly he hated it because of what it was doing to her.

He knew Kelly, and he would bet there was more to the story. She still hadn't explained to him about the boxes.

"Why are you packing?" he asked.

"That's usually what you do before you move."

His gut tightened. Move? Why? Especially now. "Just a damn minute. Bloomhurst might be able to can you, which is an issue I'll get to in a minute, but he can't run you out of town."

"Who said anything about leaving town? I'm taking an apartment on Walnut Street," she said, looking down. She folded her hands in her lap.

The movement pulled her oversized navy blue top across her gently curved abdomen. She had no business moving in her condition.

"I want the whole story, Kelly. This isn't like you. You're not exactly a spontaneous person."

"There you go with the flattery again—"

"Don't change the subject. Spit it out."

"You won't like it," she said, glancing at him.

"I already don't. How much worse can it get?"

"There's a rumor that you're the baby's father."

"What?" He sat forward. "That's the dumbest thing I ever heard. We're just friends."

She nodded. "I said you wouldn't like it. I'm pretty sure Liz McCutcheon mentioned it to Mr. Bloomhurst, but I can't say I wouldn't jump to the same conclusion myself. After all, I live a stone's throw from your front door."

"But we're just friends."

"You said that already." She sighed. "I know it and you know it, but think how the arrangement must look to everyone else. That's why I have to move."

"No, you don't." Mike was surprised at how angry he was; he didn't want Kelly to move. Not because she was pregnant and it would be hard on her and the baby, and not because he hated knuckling under to gossip-mongers, but because he liked having her across the driveway from him.

Kelly and her mother had moved in about six weeks before Mrs. Walker had died of cancer. Several years before, the woman he thought of as a second mother had refused Mike's offer of a loan to help her son, Jim, establish his accounting business in Phoenix. She had mortgaged her home instead. When she had become ill, she hadn't wanted Kelly and Jim to have to deal with a large payment, and had sold her property. Kelly had moved back from Arizona to take care of her mother, and Mike had insisted the two of them live in his empty guest house. They had agreed, but only if he would let them pay rent. After her mother had passed away, Kelly stayed. She didn't know the money went into a bank account for her. If he couldn't talk her out of moving, she might need it sooner than he'd expected.

"Don't you see, Mike? I won't let any of this hurt you. If I move, the rumors will go away."

"If people already think I'm the father, your moving won't change anything." Mike stood up and started pacing. "I'm going to see Cliff in the morning and set him straight. I'm going to get your job back and raise so much hell an 8.0 earthquake will look like a walk in the park."

"Don't, Mike. First of all, Mr. Bloomhurst was told to fire me, and it was his job to do it. Besides, he didn't start the rumor. Second, his hands are tied and he doesn't deserve to have you come down on him. I'd prefer to go quietly."

Mike saw the slight tremble of her lip, just before she caught it between her teeth. Then he saw red.

"I may not be able to do any good, but he's sure as hell going to know how I feel," he said.

"And what good will that do? What if you get fired, too?"

"I made enough money playing pro ball. I don't need their job. And I sure as hell don't need an ulcer. Someone needs to tell that uptight McCutcheon that she can't mess with people's lives."

"She can and she did. But that's my problem. If you get fired, what's going to happen to your football team in the fall? You've been teaching and training your senior players since they were freshmen. That was your first year here. They have a chance at the league title for the first time in years. You can't abandon them."

"And you're not abandoning your students?"

"I don't have a choice. You do."

"You're a gifted teacher, Kelly. You can't let a narrow-minded group of people run you off without a fight. The kids will be the real losers."

"I haven't got tenure. I have no weapons to fight with. And you're right about the kids being the losers. The football program brings in a lot of revenue. Just think what would happen if you give the community a championship."

As much as he hated to admit it, she was right. He had some talented young men who he had taken as skinny fourteen-year-olds and molded into fine players. If he left now and had to be replaced, this year's football program would be sacked big-time. It could scrap the season for these guys, and more important than that, it would affect their chances to be looked at by colleges for athletic scholarships.

"Okay, you've got a point. I won't give McCutcheon a piece of my mind." He stopped pacing and pointed at her. "Don't you dare tell me I can't spare any to give her."

"Everyone knows jocks have more muscles than brains."

For the first time since she'd let him in, Kelly laughed. The worry and frown lines were gone for a moment and it was like the sun had come out after a storm. Mike found that he wanted to chase away her clouds so she would always look sunny.

He wouldn't go to the school board, but he would find a way to help her somehow. He hated seeing her lose her job. He knew how much she wanted the baby. There must be a way she could have both. And he had to convince her that she didn't have to protect him. He didn't give a damn what people said.

She sighed. "If only I had tenure, it wouldn't be so easy to get rid of me."

"What did Cliff say to you?"

"That the school board could not allow a woman in the classroom who was pregnant and unmarried."

Mike continued to pace in front of the fireplace. "So the *M* word is the key factor here. How did you find out that people think I'm junior's father?"

"Mr. Bloomhurst told me, then came right out and asked. After that he said it was a stupid question."

"Why?"

"He said if you were the baby's father, he and I wouldn't be having the discussion at all. What do you suppose he meant by that?"

Mike knew exactly what Cliff had meant. He was surprised he hadn't thought of it himself. He came to a halt and looked at her. It was brilliant. He liked her; she liked him; they both liked kids. Why not?

"Mike, you have a strange look on your face. What are you thinking about?"

"I have it, Kelly. The perfect solution to our problem."

"It's not *our* problem. It's my problem and I'd appreciate it if you would—"

"I'd appreciate it if you would be quiet and listen to my ingenious solution."

"All right. What is the magic answer?"

"Marry me."

Chapter Two

Kelly's eyes widened. "Marry you?"

"Yes."

"This is not a joking matter, Mike. Like I said before, if you can't be supportive, then go away."

"I'm not kidding."

"Then you've been tackled one too many times without a helmet."

"There's nothing wrong with my head, Kelly. This is the right thing to do."

"Right for whom? I don't need a man to rescue me."

"You need to be married. And how you're going to do that without a man is beyond me." Mike started pacing again.

"I've sworn off men."

"Have you sworn off friends, too, Kelly?" He stopped and folded his arms over his chest. "I want to help."

"I appreciate that, Mike. But marriage?" She looked

at him helplessly. "Friends change your flat tire. They loan you five dollars to tide you over until payday. They tell you when there's lipstick on your teeth. They don't marry you because you're going to have a baby."

"Why not?" The way he was looking at her, Kelly could swear he was dead serious.

She was truly touched by Mike's gesture, but it was out of the question. "Before I try to beat some sense into you, I have a *why* of my own."

"Shoot," he said, and braced himself.

"Why would you want to get married again? Since your divorce you've been swearing that no woman would drag you down ball-and-chain lane again. So why would you do this?"

"Why should I marry thee, let me count the whys."

"You're not a poet, Mike. And you're not funny."

"I'm not trying to be funny." He put his hands on his hips. "I've got a proposition for you."

"Is this one going to be more outrageous than the last one?" She rolled her eyes, but couldn't help laughing.

"I'm going to ignore your sarcasm, Ms. Walker. How about this? If I can come up with ten good reasons why we should get married, you'll say yes to my proposal."

Kelly had him now. There was no way he could come up with one really good reason, let alone ten. "All right. You're on. Is there a time limit?"

He looked offended. "This isn't 'Jeopardy.'"

"That all depends on your point of view." She settled herself comfortably against the cushions of the couch and looked at him, waiting for him to start. "Any time you're ready. Reason number one."

He leaned a shoulder against the oak mantel and

thought for a minute. "You don't hate football. My first wife couldn't stand it, except for the so-called celebrity perks."

"Remember, these have to be good reasons."

"What's better than football? But if you don't think that's good enough, I've got nine more." He started walking back and forth in front of her. Then he stopped and said, "Okay, I've got it. If I'm married, women will leave me alone, and I won't have to beat them off with a stick. And we could use two-for-one coupons at restaurants."

"Will you stop being ridiculous? Marriage is not a prerequisite for a dinner date. And don't forget I live across the driveway. I haven't seen more than a babe or two beating a path to your door. That doesn't seem like a problem that requires this drastic a solution." She folded her arms and looked at him sternly. "I need serious, personal reasons."

"All right. What about repaying your family for taking me in as a kid when I needed discipline and guidance? What about the fact that the night before she died, I promised your mother I'd look out for you? And the fact that I didn't keep that promise or you wouldn't be in this situation now?"

His commitment to that vow touched her deeply. He was a wonderful guy and it was comforting to know she had someone like him in her corner. But she had to convince him that he wasn't to blame for everything that happened to her.

"My parents wanted you to live with us because they cared about kids and you were in trouble. They knew you'd turn out all right, all you needed was a firm hand. They were absolutely right." She placed her palm on her stomach. "My mother didn't expect you to be my keeper. I'm not your responsibility, Mike."

"Yeah? Then why do I still feel responsible? You called me the night after the funeral, right after your brother went back to Phoenix. I wasn't here."

"And I called Doug because I needed someone to talk to. What I didn't know was that he didn't have talking in mind when he came over."

"I'd still like to break his neck for taking advantage of you the way he did." Mike looked angry, furious in fact. She was surprised that he still felt that strongly after all these months.

What would he do if he knew Doug was trying to get in touch with her? He'd left messages at school and on the answering machine at home, but she hadn't returned any of his calls. For Mike's sake she decided it would be best not to tell him.

"Guilt is not a good reason to marry, Mike. Let's go at this from a different angle. What would *I* get from marrying you? Besides the obvious reason," she said looking at her stomach.

He thought for a minute. "Joint tax return. You could be the official team tutor."

"I'm that, anyway. Why would anything change?"

"Then what about a name for the baby?" he asked.

"I'll pick out names. I don't need help for that."

"No. I mean a last name."

Kelly's gaze met his, and she knew what he was thinking. Mike's mother had never married his father. In school he had gotten into fights because of what the kids had called him. "Bastard." A dirty, filthy name. All the more hurtful because it was true. He was politely telling her that if she wasn't married when her baby was born, the child would be a bastard. She felt a tightness in her chest, a small pain around her heart.

"That was hitting below the belt, Mike."

"You don't have a belt anymore, Kel."

She blinked and looked away. "You've gone from ridiculous to the Dark Ages. This is the nineties. A lot of women are choosing single parenthood."

"I may be old, but I can still remember how it feels to be different from the other kids. That hasn't changed."

"I don't want to play this game anymore." Kelly stood up and started toward the kitchen.

Mike took her arm to stop her, then turned her to him. "I'm not trying to hurt you, but there are some things you should think about. I've given you a lot of outstanding reasons why marriage is a practical solution to your situation."

"You haven't given me one that's good for you. And don't tell me about running interference for Bambi and Fawn, or the guilt factor or football. Why in the world would you want to get married?"

He sighed and dropped his hand from her arm. "As you pointed out, I'm old. Old men get tired of living alone."

Mr. Bachelor Mike Cameron tired of living alone? For just an instant she saw a trace of loneliness on his face. She'd never seen him this way and it warmed her heart that he would share that with her.

"I didn't say you were old. I said you were living in the Dark Ages."

"Means the same thing."

"All right, you're ancient and you want someone to share the rocking chair with. Why me, Mike? I'm going to have a baby. Doesn't that make you want to kick that rocker into high gear and run the other way?''

"No. You want to know why?" He looked into her eyes and she nodded. His expression told her he was being completely serious now, and that got her attention in a big way.

"We're friends, Kelly. The best. That's more than most people ever have. You know what else?" She shook her head. "It's all I ever expect to have. So that makes it pretty good."

"But it's not all I ever expect to have."

"You said you've sworn off men."

"Not forever. Someday I want to find real love, romantic love." She walked back into the kitchen to continue dismantling her personal possessions. She climbed onto a chair and reached for her cow picture with the words Feeding Time.

"What are you doing on that chair?" Mike took her elbow and helped her down. "Don't ever do that again. I'll get that stuff for you."

He reached the things she couldn't—the clock her mother had made, the brass plaque that said, "On this spot in 1897, nothing happened," and the picture of her newest words to live by, "Success is the intelligent use of mistakes."

"You're holding out for something that doesn't exist, Kelly. There's no such thing as true love."

Her eyes filled and she turned away so that he wouldn't see. "I think it exists. My parents had it. I don't want to settle for less. Thank you, Mike. Someday I'll probably kick myself for being a stupid fool. But I have to say no to your proposal."

He let out a long breath. "If you change your mind, the offer's open."

"I can't think of anything that would make me change my mind. But I appreciate it. Now, if you'll excuse me, I've got a lot to do. The apartment management company is going to check out my application and let me know in a day or two if I have the apartment."

He stacked the things he'd taken down. "You're determined to move out?"

"I think it's for the best."

He shook his head, and she expected an argument. But all he said was, "See you later, Kel."

"Good night, Mike."

The sight of him walking away, then the sound of the front door closing behind him were just about the loneliest things Kelly could imagine. She slumped into a chair and stared at nothing in particular. Mike Cameron had just asked her to marry him, and he was serious. Not only that, he was angry that she'd refused his proposal. His kindness made her heart ache. A tangle of emotion tightened her chest and clogged her throat.

She was pregnant. She was unemployed. She was moving. She was probably crazy to boot. What woman in her right mind would say no to a hunky, handsome sweetheart like Mike? Tears gathered in her eyes and she sniffled. She reminded herself that she was doing this to protect him. But she couldn't stop the single teardrop that slipped from the corner of her eye, rolled down her cheek and plopped on her chest.

If she was doing the right thing, why did it feel so wrong and so awful?

Mike was in a bad mood the next day. At football practice the players couldn't do anything right. In his office afterward, he sat behind his desk and tried to figure out why. It didn't take him long to realize that it was him, not them. He was tired. Thanks to Kelly he hadn't slept well. She had made him mad as hell. Partly because she was moving out, but mostly because she had refused to marry him.

Once the idea had taken hold, he'd really warmed to it. He wasn't quite sure why he wanted it so much until he glanced around his office. Everywhere he looked were reminders that without the Walker family, he wouldn't be where he was today. In the glass trophy case across from the door were high school, college and professional awards. There was a photograph of the football banquet during his senior year in high school when Frank Walker had insisted on giving Mike the most valuable player award. Even though the man had suffered a heart attack shortly after that night, Mike had tried never to let Frank Walker down. That had to be the reason why he wanted to marry Kelly and why he was so ticked off that she wouldn't.

Maybe his ego was bruised. But he had thought about that and was pretty sure that wasn't the case. Glancing at the wall again, he spotted a picture of him after college graduation. Kelly had talked him into attending the ceremony which he had thought a waste of time. Kelly had asked him why he didn't want to show off how smart he was. She had blitzed his cockiness when she had told him she couldn't stand guys whose IQ matched the circumference of their biceps. He respected her for that. Unfortunately he had married a woman who wasn't so discriminating.

The elbow injury that had ended his football career ended his marriage, too. The saying that things come in threes had never been more true. For him it was surprises. The first was that he hadn't really missed Carol after she left. The second was the realization that he was happier without her. The third that he hadn't liked her much.

That wasn't the case with Kelly.

He knew he would miss her if she moved. He liked having her around. He just plain liked her. The more he had thought about it, the more he was convinced that marrying her would be good for both of them. He just didn't think he could make Kelly see that.

A knock on his office door interrupted his thoughts.

"It's open," he said.

Jake Saterfield, a blond, blue-eyed, husky seventeen-year-old, walked in. He handed Mike a piece of paper. "There was only one message in your box in the office, Coach." The look on his face said he expected to be chewed out for that fact. Mike felt bad about taking out his problems on the players.

"Thanks for picking this up, Jake." The boy nodded and started to turn away. "That was a good run you had today. Keep it up and you've got a shot at breaking the school record for yards rushing."

Jake grinned. "You got it, Coach."

"How'd English go today?"

"Mrs. Wishart said she'd let me know my test grade first thing tomorrow."

"How do you think you did?"

He shrugged. "I knew most of the answers."

"Good. Hey, see you tomorrow."

"Right."

After the boy had gone, Mike checked the message. It was from the Southern California Real Estate Management Co.

He dialed the number and a woman's voice came on the line. "Miss Anderson."

He leaned back in his chair. "This is Mike Cameron. You left a message for me. I'm assuming this is about my tenant Kelly Walker?"

"That's right, Mr. Cameron. She listed you as a reference on her application for an apartment."

Mike wasn't quite sure when the idea hit him, he only knew that it seemed like a good one. If Kelly didn't have a place to go, she couldn't move.

"How long has Miss Walker been a tenant of yours, Mr. Cameron?"

"Not long." He put just a hint of disapproval in his voice.

"Oh?" He heard a hundred questions in that one syllable.

"I guess you'd like me to be specific. She's rented from me for just under eight months."

"And you've had problems with her?" The tone was definitely suspicious.

Mike reminded himself that he owed it to her family to watch out for her. He could do that better if she stayed in the guest house. He propped his feet up on his desk. He didn't like doing this to Kelly, but there were times when she was too stubborn for her own good. "I wouldn't say problems," he said, putting just a hint of hesitation in his voice. "Did you know she's pregnant?"

"Yes, she gave us that information. The building accepts children, so that's not an obstacle. Is there anything else we should know about Miss Walker?"

Mike winced, but he had to do it. "She's unemployed."

"She put on her application that she's a teacher with the Newhall High School District."

"She is, but just until the end of the school year."

"Does she have another position lined up?"

"Not that I'm aware of."

"Is there anything else that you think I should know?" she asked.

"No. I think I've said enough."

"Yes, I think you have Mr. Cameron. I appreciate your candor."

"Glad to help, Miss Anderson."

Mike hung up the phone and couldn't help feeling like he'd drop-kicked a kitten. It had been a split-second decision. He hadn't said anything that wasn't the truth. She didn't need to move out; he was doing this for her. His mouth pulled tight as he shook his head. No matter how he tried to whitewash it, he was a little surprised at how low he'd sunk. Still, a little guilt was a small price to pay. He wasn't sorry he'd sabotaged her.

Kelly carried another batch of boxes from her car into her bedroom, then went to the kitchen. The red light on her answering machine blinked twice. She pushed the button and after rewinding, a male voice came on. "Kelly? If you're there, pick up the phone. It's Doug. Either you're not there, or you're not talking to me. Probably the latter. I don't blame you, but I need to speak with you. Since you won't return my calls, I'm going to drop by. See you later."

Kelly groaned. "Great. What else could go wrong?"

Then she heard the second message. "Miss Walker, this is Leigh Anderson. I wanted to let you know the apartment you looked at has been rented, and I'm sorry to say there are no other vacancies. Give me a call if you have any questions.''

The machine clicked off and Kelly slapped the ceramic tile counter. Double whammy.

Now she would have to hunt for another apartment. That would set her back, and she didn't have time to waste. She had to move, unpack and settle, and get a nursery ready for the baby before she was too far along in her pregnancy to do it.

And as for Doug—she did *not* want to see him, later or ever again in her lifetime.

She looked at her kitchen, the boxes stacked up and empty walls where her pictures had been. ''What am I going to do?'' she asked.

The answer came instantly. She would do what she always did. She would go talk to Mike. He was her friend, and no matter what he thought about her decisions, he would always stand by her.

That was what she would miss most when she moved. She liked being able to talk to him. With a face like he had, what was not to like? But there was more to him than that or he wouldn't be her friend.

She slipped on her sneakers and walked across the driveway to his house. It was six o'clock and still light out, but there was a chill in the evening air. In another month, it would be hot, and the baby would be bigger. Everyone said summer was the worst time to give birth. As far as she was concerned, her timing on that was the only thing that had gone right. School was out and she could resume teaching in September. She was sorry she wouldn't be at Stevenson, but she thought maybe a private school would hire her. She planned to submit applications in the next day or so.

She stood on Mike's brick porch and rang the bell.

While she waited for him to answer, she straightened her floral maternity top over the matching stretch pants.

A second before Mike opened the door, a shadow on the beveled glass told her he was there. Then the flesh-and-blood man filled the doorway. Kelly's heart skipped a little at the sight of him. The feeling was happening with more frequency, but she chalked it up to hormones. Pregnancy wreaked havoc on a woman's body. Why couldn't she have a normal, physical reaction to a good-looking man? When her hormones settled down, so would the feeling.

"Kelly, what are you doing here? What's wrong?"

"What makes you think there's something wrong?"

One of Mike's dark eyebrows lifted and there was a strange look on his face. If she didn't know better, she would have sworn he was expecting her.

"You just look funny," he said.

That made sense. She felt funny, too. "I just wanted to talk to you. May I come in?"

"Sure." He opened the door wider and stepped back to allow her inside.

Kelly loved his house. She knew he had hired a decorator, but his touch was there, too. The hardwood floor in the entryway where she stood, the oak-trimmed doorways around the kitchen straight ahead and the beige carpet in the living room to her left, he had insisted on those touches. There was a masculine air to the place mainly because of the lack of frills, flowers and froo-froo. It had a tangible solidness, like Mike. He was forthright and honest; he would never do anything shady or underhanded.

"Have you eaten dinner yet?" he asked.

She shook her head. "Do you have an extra frozen dinner?"

"Yup. Hungry man size. Think you can handle it?" One corner of his mouth lifted in a smile that was guaranteed to affect female hearts on the spot. Hers was no exception.

"I think so. After all, I'm eating for two."

She followed him into the kitchen and sat on one of the tall stools at the bar that separated the work area from the breakfast nook behind her.

Mike opened the freezer and pulled out a couple of dinners. "Chicken and mashed potatoes all right?" When she nodded, he read the directions and popped it into the microwave. "What did you want to talk to me about?"

"They rented my apartment to someone else."

"Really?" he said, his back to her.

"Yeah. It's not the only place in town, but two-bedroom units aren't that easy to find in a security building that takes children and has an enclosed yard."

He punched some buttons, and the oven began to hum. He turned around. "You look puzzled."

"There's a good reason for that. I don't understand what happened."

"What do you mean?"

"When I looked at the apartment, Miss Anderson acted as if the place was already mine, and the background check was merely a formality. Today her manner was definitely cooler. Did she call you?"

"As a matter of fact, she did," he admitted.

"What did she say?"

"She asked how long you had been my tenant and I told her. She said she knew about the baby."

Kelly nodded. "I wanted to be up-front about that. It didn't seem to be a problem."

"You're taking this too personally. They probably

had more than one application. I'd bet the other was from dinks.''

She frowned. ''That's not a very nice thing to say.''

''D.I.N.K.—double income no kids.''

''Oh.'' She thought about that for a moment. Someone like that would be a better risk than a Q.I.B.O.W. Questionable income, baby on way. ''Maybe you're right.''

''I'm sure I am. You want something to drink?''

She nodded. ''I want a glass of wine.''

He frowned. ''No alcohol for pregnant ladies.''

''I know that. I just said I wanted it. What have you got that I can have?''

Mike turned away and looked in the refrigerator. ''I have milk, apple juice, soda or water.''

''Juice please,'' she said.

Kelly wondered if this was what it would feel like to be married. Eating dinner together, relating the events of the day, not being alone. It was nice. Mike's concern about her condition touched her, too, and a sense of wistfulness washed over her. To have someone to share things with—the baby's movement, the results of her monthly doctor visits, heartburn, her fears about the birth, her fears about a roof over her head. But it was a fantasy.

At least for now. Someday she would find a man who would sweep her off her feet, and she would have all the love she'd dreamed about. That goal was merely delayed, not unobtainable.

Mike set a glass of apple juice in front of her. He leaned his forearms on the cream-colored tiles and met her gaze. ''You know, Kel, you don't have to move.''

''Yes, I do. It's not fair that you be dragged into this situation.''

"Whether you like it or not, I'm in it because I'm your friend."

She put her hand on his arm. The little jolt she got from the contact with his warm skin surprised her. The slight flicker she saw in Mike's eyes made her wonder if he'd felt something, too. She glanced down at her fingers on his forearm. Why had she never noticed before how tan he was compared to her? How wide and strong his wrists were? Must be that hormone thing again. Maybe it made a woman's powers of observation more acute. Whatever the side effects, it would be best to ignore the sensation. She took her hand away and curled her fingers around her glass.

"Mike, I don't want to argue with you. I've made up my mind to move. Can't we just drop it?"

He nodded. "We can if you'll promise not to make a hasty decision. You've got a home as long as you want one. Don't do anything stupid."

"Me?" she said, pressing her palm to her chest in mock amazement. "However can you say that? Just because I'm pregnant—"

"That sorry son of a bitch took advantage of you." Mike stood up straight and his dark eyes smoldered with anger.

"It's not all his fault."

"If he was any kind of man, he would never have pressed you under the circumstances. Good God, you'd just buried your mother."

"Don't forget I called him," she said.

"Why are you defending him?"

"I'm not. I'm trying to be fair." She looked down into the golden liquid in her glass.

"There's something else, isn't there? What is it, Kelly?"

She glanced up quickly. "How do you always know?"

"I've known you a long time. Tell me what's going on."

"Doug's been calling me for the last couple weeks."

Mike tensed. "What does he want?"

"I haven't talked to him. He's just left messages. I got another one today."

"What did he say?"

"He's coming over tonight."

Chapter Three

"For God's sake, Kelly, why didn't you say so before?"

The microwave beeped loudly, and Mike took out the dinner. He pulled back the plastic and felt as hot as the steam escaping. He couldn't believe she had waited this long to tell him that the guy was harassing her.

As his anger grew, adrenaline pumped through him. He hadn't liked Doug the first time he'd met him. After what he'd done to Kelly, he promised himself if he ever saw the jerk again, he would make him wish he'd never been born.

As if sensing his mood, Kelly shifted on the bar stool. "I didn't tell you sooner because I hadn't planned to tell you at all. Forget it. I'll handle Doug."

"If there's anything left of him when I get through, you're welcome to it."

Kelly's eyes widened. "When did you develop these

Neanderthal tendencies? This is a side of you I've never seen before.''

Mike wasn't sure himself why he felt this way. He hadn't wanted to deck a guy over a girl since high school. But the fact was Kelly was going through hell because of Doug Hammond and Mike wanted his pound of flesh—or to pound Doug's flesh. He didn't much care which. ''When will he be here?''

''He didn't say.'' She took a sip of her juice.

''Doesn't matter. I'll just hang around and take care of him.''

Kelly put down the glass, and when she looked at him irritation was written all over her face.

''This is my problem, Mike. I appreciate your friendship more than you'll ever know, but it's not a license to butt into my life. When he gets here, I'll listen to what he has to say, then I'll send him on his way.''

Mike understood her wanting to do this on her own; that was the kind of woman Kelly was. He just couldn't get over the feeling that it would be like leaving a defenseless lamb to the big bad wolf.

''Can I just be there when you see him?'' he asked.

''No.''

''What if I promise not to say anything?''

She snorted. ''Fat chance of that.''

''What if—''

''No. You can't stay. Besides, don't you have a football meeting tonight?''

He started to shake his head, then stopped when he realized she was right. ''Geez, with all this other stuff going on, I forgot. It's 'meet the coaches' night.'' He folded his arms across his chest and looked at her. ''I'll just have to miss it.''

''You can't. This is when you take advantage of parental enthusiasm. Dean can't pull the volunteers out of the crowd the way you can."

Dean Thompson, his assistant coach, was a gifted tactician and terrific with the players. But Kelly was right. When it came to the parents, Mike was better at getting them to become involved. The program depended heavily on that. He couldn't miss the meeting.

"Mike, don't worry about me. I'm a big girl. I can take care of myself."

"I don't like it," he grumbled, as he put the other dinner in the microwave. "But I guess there's nothing I can do."

"You're sweet to worry about me."

He turned back to her. "I'll tell you what's sweet. Remember that move Jim and I taught you before your very first date?"

She grinned. "Remember it? I got to use it that night. Do *you* remember who fixed me up with that octopus?"

"Everyone's entitled to a minor error in judgment."

"Minor?"

"He was here for the weekend. He was lonely. It was supposed to be dinner and a movie. How did I know he was going to come on to you?" He looked at her. "Just promise me one thing…"

"What?"

"Before the jerk gets here, practice that move."

"I will," she said, laughing.

The sound surrounded him and he grinned, surprised at how contagious her laughter was. As ticked off as he'd been a minute before, he was sure no one but Kelly could have made him smile.

When Kelly had first found out about the baby, she'd misplaced *her* smile for a while. Recently she'd found it, and if Hammond did anything to make her lose it again, Mike would hunt him down and take his pound of flesh. The man would never hurt Kelly again.

Kelly tensed when she heard the car pull up in front of her house. She knew the sound. It brought back painful memories of all the nights she'd expected to hear it, then waited in vain for Doug to show up. She remembered the flimsy excuses she'd believed because she'd desperately wanted to. She would never forget the disillusionment of learning about his lies, his other women, *after* she found out she was going to have a baby.

There was nothing he could tell her now that she wanted to hear. She had nothing to say to him. Period. This should be a very short meeting. But she would feel a lot more confident if she could stop the butterflies in her stomach or the trembling in her hands.

She opened the door as he strode up the walkway. He smiled at her. "Hello, Kelly."

"Doug." She motioned him inside.

He had the lanky good looks of a male model in a pin-striped suit. The red tie he wore was perfectly knotted at the collar of his crisp white shirt. His sandy hair was slightly mussed, and his hazel eyes held an expression that said he was glad to see her. She didn't believe it.

She frowned at him. "What do you want?"

"That's pretty cold," he said, raising an eyebrow.

"The last time we spoke, you made it clear that you wanted nothing to do with the baby or me. I have no reason to think that the situation's changed. So I'd like to know what you want."

Doug looked sheepish. "I'm sorry about that, Kel—"

"Don't call me that," she snapped.

"All right. I just wanted you to know that I'm sorry about the things I said. The situation caught me off guard and I—I suppose I sort of panicked."

"You?" Kelly shook her head at his smoothness. He was as cool as they came. She had found out the hard way how he could lie without batting an eye. "Panicked?"

"Believe it or not," he said in that affable, self-effacing way that had charmed her once. "You don't know what it's like to hear that you're going to be a father."

"That's typical, Doug. It's always about you. Did you stop to think how I felt finding out I was going to be a mother?"

"That's why I'm here now."

Her eyes widened and she wanted to laugh in his face, or slap it. "I'm six months pregnant. Took you long enough." Her chest tightened with anger. "During all that time did you think about what would happen to me? Whether or not this would affect my life, my job?"

"Has it?"

"You bet it has, buster. I don't have a job as of June."

His eyebrows pulled together and, if she didn't know better, she would have thought he was genuinely sorry.

"Then it's fortunate I'm here."

"Why?"

"Kelly, I want you to marry me. I want to be a father to our child."

Kelly's jaw dropped. She didn't know what she had expected him to say, but it certainly wasn't this.

Her reaction was knee-jerk, and she should have put it exactly where Mike and her brother had taught her. Instead, she clasped her shaking hands together and tried to control her astonishment, then the surge of anger that followed.

"I wouldn't marry you if you were the last man on earth."

There was no reaction on his face, no indication whether her words had hurt him or not. "Think about this carefully. You just said you'll be out of a job come June. How are you going to support yourself, let alone a kid?"

A kid? The baby was just an impersonal, nuisance kid as far as he was concerned. She didn't want him anywhere near her child, not to mention raising him. "I'll work it out. Alone," she added firmly.

"If you marry me, I can take care of you both. I'm up for a partnership in the law firm—"

"I smell a rat," she said, her eyes narrowing. With time and distance, she had realized Doug never did anything for anyone else unless there was something in it for him. Besides, he'd never said a word about loving her. If she hadn't been so upset, it would have been funny. Two proposals in two days. Must be some kind of record for a pregnant lady. She'd been tempted to take Mike up on his offer, but Doug's left her cold.

He looked down for a moment, then met her suspicious gaze. "You know the firm is very conservative and traditional. I don't want to say that I'm not concerned about my success. But that's not the reason I asked you—"

"Stuff a sock in it, Doug. Of course that's the reason.'' She took a deep breath. "Now I want you to listen, because I'm only going to say this once. I should have known that a lawyer who would sleep with his client couldn't be trusted. You're a liar and I'd be a fool to ever trust you again. There's nothing you could say that would persuade me to marry you.''

He frowned, and there was a look in his eyes that sent a chill down her spine. "Then you leave me no alternative. I'll have to sue you for custody of my child.''

"What?'' She took a step toward him, her heart pounding furiously. "Why? You don't want this child. Good Lord, you said I should get rid of it, and if I didn't, I shouldn't expect any help from you.''

"I've changed my mind.''

"For your own selfish reasons. But I don't understand how taking my baby would help you improve your standing in the firm.''

"The only thing they like better than a stable family man is a cause. And if that cause involves a baby, they would eat it up.'' His eyebrows pulled together thoughtfully. "I don't recall a recent case where a father sued the pregnant mother for his child. It would generate a lot of publicity.''

"You're bluffing. Why would you waste the time and effort? No judge would take a baby from its mother.''

"He might if that mother is unmarried, unemployed and the father is well-off financially. Who do you think would be the better risk?''

Fear clutched at her, and Kelly had never wanted anything in her life more than she wanted him gone.

"You're despicable. I think you should leave now, Doug.'' She pointed to the front door and was angry when she saw that her hand was shaking. She lowered it to her side and steadied her voice until it was as cool and calm as she could make it. "Get out. And don't make the mistake of coming back."

Doug walked over to the door and opened it. "Think about what I said, Kelly. It would be in both our best interests and the baby's if you married me. The alternative is... Well," he shrugged.

Her heart pounded so hard it hurt. "If you dare try to take my baby—"

"Just think about it," he said.

"Get out of my sight."

When the door closed behind him, Kelly sank onto the sofa. "What am I going to do?" she asked. There was no answer in that empty room.

After the meeting, Mike made his way up the driveway in his Bronco. Everything had gone well. There were a lot of spirited parents of incoming ninth-graders who would get involved and keep the program running. And he would have them for four years.

From the moment he left home, he had been anxious to get back, and the night had dragged. It was just past ten-thirty. Every time he had tried to slip out the door, another parent had stopped him to talk. He hoped he had said the right things; he couldn't remember. Because his mind was on Kelly and her meeting with Doug. The man was a double-dealing, back-stabbing, lying, cheating son of a bitch and he was up to no good. The guy wanted something, and whatever he was after, Mike was certain Kelly wouldn't like it.

As he drove closer to the house, the headlights picked out a figure huddled on his front porch. She looked up and stood. Kelly!

There was a screech of brakes as Mike stopped the car, then killed the engine. He threw open the door and jumped out. In three strides he was beside her.

"What is it, Kelly? Did he hurt you? What are you doing out here?"

"He didn't hurt me. I just couldn't stand to be in the same room where he'd been."

"Why? What's wrong? What did he say?"

"H-he's going to take my b-baby—" She was shaking.

"He's what?"

"He's going to sue me for custody—" Her chattering teeth forced her to stop.

"He's not going to take anything. You're cold. I'm going to take you inside and get you warm. Then you can start at the beginning and tell me what's going on."

Mike put his arm around her and led her into his house. He sat her on the plaid sofa in his family room. Although it was May, the night was still cool enough for a fire, and he lit one in the fireplace beside them.

He turned and looked at her. "If you weren't pregnant I'd give you a brandy."

"If I weren't pregnant, I wouldn't be in this mess." She scooted forward, closer to the flames, and held her hands out as she rubbed them together for warmth.

"I'll make you some hot chocolate." When she nodded, he crossed to the kitchen and put a mug of cold milk in the microwave. After he punched in the numbers, it began to hum and he put his arms on the bar as he studied Kelly.

Firelight flickered over her shadowed face. Her mouth was tight and her eyes drawn. She was taut and tense, strung as tightly as a high school football team before the cross town game for local bragging rights.

Mike kicked himself for leaving her alone tonight. If only he'd been there....

When the hot chocolate was ready, he took it to her and grabbed the blue-and-green afghan she'd made him that was resting on the sofa back. He spread it across her knees and handed her the cup. Then he sat down beside her. He put his arm around her and pulled her against his side. Just to warm her, he thought, although there was a part of him that noticed she felt nice there. He pushed the idea away.

"Now, what's going on?" he asked.

"I told you, he wants to sue me for—" She stopped and took a deep breath, then wrapped her hands around her mug. "I'll start at the beginning. He asked me to marry him."

Mike was stunned. "You said no, didn't you?"

"Of course." She shook her head angrily as she thought for a moment. "I'm *so* stupid."

"For saying no?"

"For letting it slip that I'm losing my job. He's going to take the baby away from me because he wants a partnership in the law firm. I can't support myself and the baby. He's a lawyer. I'm afraid the judge will give him the baby."

"Honey, you're not making a lot of sense."

"I know. I'm sorry. I've been thinking and waiting for you for hours. I've racked my brain for a way out. I've come up with something. It's the only thing I can think of."

"What is it?"

"You said if I changed my mind the offer was still open." She looked at him warily. "Mike, I need a man."

"You've sworn off men."

"Only temporarily. I just need you for a little while."

Tears glistened in her eyes, and at that moment he would have said anything or done anything for her.

"Are you asking me to marry you?" he asked.

She nodded.

He probably should have been surprised, but he wasn't. He had come up with ten good reasons why marriage would solve her problems, and he still thought it was a good idea. She had turned him down flat because she wanted romantic love someday. But Hammond had shoved her over the edge with his threats, tipping the scale in Mike's favor. If it was just her own welfare, she would never have come to him. But her child was in jeopardy. Mike could give her what she needed most, the security of his name and the money to show that creep that he couldn't threaten her and take the baby.

"All right. I'll marry you."

She looked into the dark circle of her hot chocolate and continued as if she hadn't heard him. "It's the only way. If you marry me, I'll get to keep my job. Not only that, but in a custody hearing, surely a couple would look better than a bachelor. Especially one like Doug—"

"I said all right. I'll marry you." He lifted her chin with his knuckle, forcing her gaze up to his. Wonder swirled in her eyes.

"You will? Are you sure?"

He nodded. "I asked you first. Remember?"

"Yes."

"Are you absolutely sure this is what you want to do? If you have any doubts, we can find another way," he said.

She shook her head. "I'm sure. Unless you've changed your mind," she said quickly. "After all, Mike, this isn't your problem. The baby's not yours. Doesn't that bother you?"

He stared into the fire for a few moments. By asking him to marry her, she had made him happier than he'd been in a long time. He wasn't sure why, and he didn't want to question it. Because he didn't want to think about the basic rule of his belief system: Good things don't last. That wasn't important now. He needed to reassure Kelly that everything would work out fine.

"Kelly, let's get one thing straight. This baby is yours. You're my friend. How can I not care about your child? Wouldn't you feel the same about mine?"

"Of course I would," she said. "I see your point."

"There's one more thing. When the baby's born, I want your married name on his birth certificate."

She looked at him, and there was a suspicious brightness in her eyes. "I've never seen you like this before," she said. "You're willing to marry me so that my child won't go through what you did?"

"No one will ever call this kid that name. Not if I have anything to say about it."

For years Mike had tried to bury the pain of a hundred childhood taunts, but he couldn't quite hide it from Kelly. For some reason he didn't mind that she knew.

"Mike, you're quite a guy. Promise me one thing?" she asked, her voice slightly huskier than normal. He hoped she wasn't going to cry.

"What?"

"Promise me that whatever happens you'll always be my best friend."

That was easy. "I promise that nothing will ever stand in the way of our friendship."

"So we have a deal?" she asked. She cleared her throat, but not before he heard the emotion that had gathered there. "We're going to get married?"

"We do, and we are." Didn't people usually shake hands or something to seal a bargain?

As she looked up at him, her eyes big and green and grateful, something caught in Mike's chest. Her lips were full and looked soft and sweet. Hardly realizing what he was doing, Mike lowered his mouth to hers.

The touch sparked a warmth inside him that had nothing to do with the fire. When he pulled back, a frown puckered Kelly's forehead, and her body went rigid as if she was trying to pull away from him. Had she felt it, too?

It? There was no "it" to feel. They were just friends, best friends getting married for the sake of the baby. This was the right thing to do. That's all there was to that.

"I think we should talk about the rules," Kelly said. She slipped sideways, out of his embrace, then sat cross-legged on the couch, facing him.

"What rules?" he asked, crossing his arms.

"Maybe *rules* isn't the right word. This is an agreement." Her gaze rested on his mouth for a second, and her eyes widened slightly before she looked away. "We need to agree about some things."

"Like what?"

"Like how long the marriage will last," she said.

They hadn't even said "I do" yet and she was talking about ending it. Mike wasn't sure why, but he found that irritating.

"As long as there's any threat of him taking the baby, we need to be together."

She frowned. "You're right, of course, but that's pretty vague. I don't want you to put your life on hold for me indefinitely."

Was she concerned about him or herself? Mike wondered. "Don't worry about me."

She glanced up at him and her expression was troubled. "But I do. You're my friend and I would never do anything to jeopardize that."

"What do you suggest?"

She thought for a minute. "As long as my job is secure, I can meet Doug on equal ground in any court. I can be divorced and teach. I just can't be pregnant and unmarried. So what if we say four months? Until the beginning of school in September?"

"Won't people wonder at such a short time?"

She shrugged. "It happens all the time. Some couples stay married a matter of weeks."

If that's what she wanted, he would agree. But he wasn't sure about it. "All right, four months. But I think we should keep our defenses in reserve. We can always renegotiate and stay together longer if he's still making noises about custody."

"It's also possible that he'll have his precious partnership. If that's the case, I'm sure he won't want me or the baby, and you and I will be free to go our separate ways."

Mike frowned. He couldn't shake the feeling that jarred him every time she mentioned separating. He didn't want to think that far into the future. "We should get married as soon as possible. If he starts throwing his weight around, we'll have the grounds to bury him."

"I agree."

"Tomorrow we can get the blood tests and then the license. I'll contact a lawyer—"

"A lawyer?" Her gaze snapped up to his. "Why?"

"A college buddy of mine specializes in family law. We need expert advice on how to beat Hammond at his own game. If he starts making things ugly for you, I want to be able to stop him in his tracks."

"Oh, you're right. Of course."

"Did you think I meant something else?"

"I thought you were talking about a pre-nuptial agreement."

"It never crossed my mind," he said truthfully.

"I wouldn't blame you if you did want one. After Carol…" She glanced at him, judging his reaction. She seemed to decide correctly that he wasn't sensitive about that and went on. "I want it understood that when we split up, I don't want anything from you, Mike. You're saving my job and giving my baby a name. How can I ever repay you?"

"I'm not asking for anything except the opportunity to help. Now, we should set a date."

She let out a deep breath, looking nervous suddenly. "You pick."

"What about this Saturday?"

Her eyes grew wide, but she only said, "Can we get everything together by then?"

"I'm sure we can." He thought for a minute. "Unless you wanted something bigger than just a few friends—"

"Under the circumstances a small, quiet ceremony would be best."

"We'll need people to stand up with us."

She nodded. "I'll see if Susan would be willing to be my matron of honor. What about you?"

"I think I'll ask Cliff Bloomhurst," he said, grinning. "If he's a witness, there can't be any doubt about the fact that you'll be Mrs. Mike Cameron. And any doubts about your job should be put to rest."

She smiled back at him. "You're evil, Mike Cameron. And I mean that in the nicest possible way," she added.

"So everything's settled?" he asked.

"Saturday it is."

Chapter Four

"I now pronounce you man and wife. You may kiss your bride." The gray-haired judge looked at Kelly and Mike over the reading glasses anchored on the end of his nose.

Kelly had just become Mrs. Mike Cameron and promised to love, honor and cherish him for as long as she lived. She felt more like a fraud than a bride.

She and Mike were standing in his backyard beneath a white latticework arch covered with ivy. Shadows of early evening crept across the grass as a soft breeze rippled the cream chiffon hem of her dress and the matching veil that fell over her face to her chin. In his traditional black tuxedo, Mike looked more handsome than she'd ever seen him.

If all the guests at the wedding wouldn't think she had gone off the deep end, Kelly would have hiked up the long skirt on her chiffon dress and run as fast as she could in the other direction. But it was too late now. Besides, she still had the baby to think about.

The judge cleared his throat loudly, reminding her she still had to kiss the groom. Mike turned to her, lifted the lace in front of her eyes and winked. She knew he was trying to put her at ease as well as warning her to make this good.

On her left was Susan Wishart her matron of honor. Mike's best man, Cliff Bloomhurst, stood beside him, beaming. They believed she had married Mike because they were in love and always had been. Until now, their timing had been wrong. She couldn't blow that romantic notion by refusing to kiss him, no matter how much she wanted to do just that.

They had shared their first kiss a week ago, and the memory of it still made her body hum. Pretty scary stuff. But this was her wedding. The guests would wonder, if she didn't kiss Mike. If she tried really hard, maybe she wouldn't enjoy it so much this time.

Kelly trembled as Mike took her in his arms. He whispered so that only she could hear, "Put your arms around my neck."

She did and he smiled, a very satisfied masculine smile. She was fascinated by the flash of white teeth against his tanned face. Why had she never noticed the way the lines near his mouth deepened when he grinned? Then it was too late to notice more. He claimed her mouth with his own. The touch was gentle and sweet. Until he tightened his hold on her and deepened the kiss, warming to his task. *Warm* was definitely the word.

Liquid heat poured through her. Her knees melted like ice cubes in hot Jell-o, and if he hadn't been holding her, she would have dissolved into a puddle at his feet. When applause, whistles and approving laughter erupted around them, Kelly pulled out of his arms. She took a deep breath as Susan handed her the bridal bouquet comprised of white roses, orchids and baby's breath that Mike had surprised her with just before the ceremony. Should it worry her that on top of something old, something new, something borrowed and something blue, she had forgotten flowers, too? Or should she be more concerned that Mike had thought of everything? She didn't have time to care as the judge cleared his throat.

"Ladies and gentlemen," he said. "I present to you Mr. and Mrs. Mike Cameron."

"Mrs. Cameron," Mike said, holding out his arm.

Kelly took it and let him lead her to the covered brick patio. They had invited about twenty close friends to the six p.m. wedding, and all of them gathered around to congratulate the newly married couple. Mike excused himself and quietly talked to a distinguished-looking man standing by the open French doors. The next thing she knew, platters of hors d'oeuvres appeared, as well as waiters bearing trays of flute glasses filled with champagne. Again she was amazed that he had thought of everything.

All week she had pleaded with him to let her help. All week he had told her everything was under control and to just take it easy. She would've been able to do that if he hadn't added, "Our wedding will be perfect, down to the last detail."

They had agreed this marriage was a function of friendship. She had a sneaking suspicion that he was injecting it with something more personal. Like that kiss. The only thing more intimate than his mouth-to-mouth technique was what happened *in* the marriage bed. And that thought had kept her on edge all week. She had wanted to settle the sleeping arrangements but there had never been time. When she had seen Mike in between his wedding errands, they'd had other decisions to make. In a few hours, she had to face it.

"What's the matter? You look like you just remembered that you forgot to shut off the water in the bathtub." Susan Wishart, a tall, attractive blonde with curly hair, grinned down at her. "Is this where the enormity of the step you've taken has finally sunk in?"

"You don't know how right you are."

Her friend was far too intuitive for Kelly's peace of mind. She felt slimy again for keeping the real reasons for the marriage secret.

"The worst is over," Susan said. "Now it's time to kick off your shoes, relax and have some fun. This food looks great," she said, plucking a stuffed celery stalk from a passing tray.

Relax? Easy for you to say, Kelly thought. Facing the night alone with Mike wasn't exactly snooze city. Since the evening she and Mike had agreed to get married, she had carefully observed him. More and more she was realizing how attractive he truly was, that she could easily be susceptible to his looks and charm. It was just because of the pregnancy, she told herself. Her belly was getting bigger, and if her response to Mike was anything to go by, her reactions were getting bigger, too. Everything about her was getting bigger, including her hormones.

It was all so confusing. Over the years she had seen Mike in various stages of undress. In fact she'd seen him once stark naked, and she'd never been overly attracted. But lately she couldn't seem to stop thinking about him. And today, the way he looked in that tuxedo, the way he had kissed her, the way awareness of his masculinity hummed through her, she wasn't sure she could keep from crossing the line of friendship into something else.

Still, she tried to look at the bright side. If her re-action to him was simply a result of her body chem-istry, then it would pass as soon as the baby was born. She was determined that nothing would complicate the perfect friendship she had with him.

That decided, she relaxed a little and smiled at Su-san. "Mike did a great job with everything, didn't he?"

"That's an understatement. Especially as fast as the whole thing happened. Kelly, can I ask you some-thing?"

"What?" Kelly asked, as people milled around eat-ing and talking.

"Well, Cliff will kill me for telling you, but there are two rumors circulating. The first is that Mike is the baby's father. Which I know is not true."

"I heard that one. What's the second?"

"That he married you to help you keep your job."

"Completely untrue," Kelly said, grabbing a pastry-covered cocktail wienie from the waiter's tray to hide her flushed cheeks.

"I didn't think so, but things did happen fast after McCutcheon got into the act. But I knew there was more to it. A person would have to be deaf, dumb and blind not to see that there's something special between you and Mike."

"And let's hope marriage doesn't spoil it." Kelly said under her breath.

"What was that?"

"Nothing," she said.

Kelly wished she could confess the real reason be-hind their whirlwind wedding. But she and Mike had decided to keep Doug's threat quiet. If they had to go to court, they didn't want anyone questioning the timing of their marriage in connection with a custody battle. To all outward appearances, they had to be a deliriously in love, happily married couple.

Susan sighed. "This is the most romantic spur-of-the-moment wedding I've ever seen."

"As romantic as it can be when the bride is six months pregnant," Kelly said, brushing a hand over her rounded stomach.

"That's exactly the reason it's so romantic. He's your knight in shining armor, your Sir Walter Raleigh, throwing his cloak over the puddle of public opinion, putting to rest the vicious lies and innuendo threatening the woman he loves."

Kelly laughed. "You've been teaching English literature too long."

"With a name like Wishart what else would I teach?"

"It's about time they moved you to the biology department. A good frog dissection would do wonders for you. The formaldehyde fumes would take the stars out of your eyes."

"I'm serious. Mike's a real sweetie. Do you know how lucky you are?"

"Lucky? Who's lucky?" Mike asked, as he slipped an arm around Kelly's ever-expanding waist.

"Kelly is," Susan said.

"You mean because I decided against the Chapel of Love in Vegas?"

"The what?" Kelly asked, looking up at him. She couldn't help laughing at the feigned innocence on his face.

"You know, in the big hotels, there's always this little room off to the side with a neon rose over the doorway and baskets of white plastic flowers lining the aisle, just behind the plastic chain, and the plastic chairs in front of the plastic preacher and the plastic Presley—''

"Enough," Kelly said, groaning.

"I made up the plastic Presley because I know how you love alliteration," he said.

"Is everything really plastic?" Susan asked.

"Maybe not the preacher," he said.

"In our case, artificial might have been more appropriate," Kelly mumbled. Far from feeling lucky at the moment, she struggled with her conscience that refused to stay dormant.

Susan frowned at her. "What's wrong with you?"

"I'm sorry. Guess I have to plead fatigue. It's been a long, stressful week."

"Yeah," Mike agreed. "It's not every day you walk down Ball-and-Chain Lane."

"That's a terrible thing to say!" Susan exclaimed.

Mike shrugged. "Don't look at me. Kelly coined the phrase."

"I was quoting you," she said, defending herself.

"Isn't she feisty?" he asked, grinning. "That's one of the things I like best about her." He kissed her quickly on the lips. When he lifted his head, there was an expression in his eyes that made her very uneasy. It was a fierce—and she'd swear almost hungry—look, the farthest thing from friendly she could imagine. Especially since it curled her toes and made her heart race.

"Don't call me feisty. And don't even think about *spunky*," she said. She tried to sound stern, but the breathless quality she heard in her voice kept it from coming out that way.

"I think it's time for dinner," he said. "Let's go inside."

As she let him lead her to the dining room, Kelly reminded herself, *It's just hormones.* In two and a half months, the problem would no longer exist. That was the good news. The bad news—she was very much afraid her feelings for Mike could get out of control, even in that short a time.

Barefoot and pregnant.

Mike studied Kelly, standing on the hardwood floor in the open doorway saying goodbye to the Wisharts. He folded his arms across the accordion pleats on his now-wrinkled, formal shirt. Hours ago he'd discarded the jacket and rolled his sleeves up. Kelly had slipped out of her shoes. She stood there now, leaning against the doorjamb, rubbing one small, delicate, nylon clad foot over her other ankle.

It was one hell of a sexy look.

"Come on, Susan, it's *really* time to go." Brad Wishart took his wife's hand to lead her outside. The same height as his wife, the bearded man with gray-streaked black hair tugged her once. "We've been standing here for a long time. Another five minutes and we'll make the Guinness Book for goodbyes."

"Do you have to go so soon?" Kelly asked.

Mike slanted a quick look at her. If he didn't know better, he would swear there was a note of desperation in her voice.

"No." Susan grinned at her husband as if she was setting him up for something.

"For God's sake, Suse, they just got married. They want to be alone. You see Kelly every day at school.

You can talk to her on Monday. Let's leave them alone.''

"You mean for—" Susan stopped and lifted one eyebrow provocatively.

"Don't say it," her husband said, pointing a finger at her.

"All right." Susan gave Kelly a hug and kissed Mike on the cheek. "I wish you both many happy years together. Good night, Mr. and Mrs. Cameron."

"Good night," they both said together.

After the Wisharts were gone, Kelly shut the heavy oak door and leaned her back against it. As she looked up at Mike, all big green eyes, and a tired, troubled expression on her face, he knew something was wrong.

"What is it?" he asked.

"It bothers me a lot that we're deceiving everyone. We're only going to be together a matter of months, not years. And as far as happy—"

He pointed at her. "Don't you say it. There's no reason the time we're together can't be pleasant and even fun."

She slanted him a suspicious look. "What do you mean by fun?"

Definitely nervous about something, he thought. "Forget I said that. We won't have any fun. This is Ball-and-Chain Lane. No fun, I promise. How could I have been so stupid as to insinuate friends could have fun?"

She smiled a little and tucked her hair behind her ears then glanced to her left, into the living room where wedding gifts were stacked. "I feel like such a fraud, Mike. I can't face opening gifts."

"We have to. People will expect thank you notes.

And we can't just send a generic. You have to say thanks for the meatloaf maker or whatever the widget.''

She sighed. "You're right. I know. But would you mind if we do it in the morning? I'll come back—"

"Where are you going?"

"Home."

"This *is* your home," he said, holding his arms wide.

"I don't want to cramp your style."

"What style? I don't have a style to cramp."

"Just because we're married doesn't mean we have to live together. There's a perfectly good house across the driveway—"

"Won't work." He tucked his fingers in his tuxedo pockets as he tried to control his irritation.

"Why not?"

"Looks bad for a happily married couple to sleep in separate houses."

"Who will know?"

"You never had anyone drop in on you?" he asked.

"Well," she hedged.

"Happens to me all the time. Or what if you get a phone call?"

"You could ask them to hold on and run across the driveway to get me."

"I'm not going to live like an episode of 'I Love Lucy.' What's wrong, Kel?"

"Nothing."

"Yeah, and I'm Princess Di. Are you afraid to sleep with me? No, not even with me, to be in the same house with me?"

"How could I be afraid of you?"

"I don't know, but you are. You afraid you'll get pregnant?"

"Very funny."

"Then what is it?"

"All of my things are still over there. We agreed our marriage would be only for a few months. Seems like a waste of time and energy to move everything down here, then back when we split—"

"Geez. We said 'I do' four hours ago, and not only are you talking about the end, you're acting like I've got the plague."

"I'm sorry, Mike. I don't mean to."

"If even one person believes this is not a real marriage, it could get ugly."

"Define *real*." She bit the corner of her lip, and her eyes grew wider as they filled with doubt. She'd never looked at him with anything but trust, teasing or laughter. He didn't like what she was thinking.

"We've joked about jocks being Neanderthals with too many hands. But let's get something straight here and now. I would never push my advantage. I'm not like Doug—"

"Oh, Mike," she said, moving forward. She put her hand on his arm and looked up at him, contrition written all over her face. "I didn't mean to imply that. You're my best friend. I know better than anyone that you're nothing like him. It's not you I'm worried about. It's m—" She stopped and her eyes widened more if possible.

"It's what?" he asked.

"That's not important."

"It is to me. I'm your friend. This is your home for as long as you want or need one for yourself and the baby. I want you to be comfortable with me."

"I am."

He snorted. "Yeah. About as comfortable as a quarterback looking at a safety blitz."

"I don't quite know what that means, but I sense that you're having some trouble believing me."

"It means the other team sends about eight hundred pounds of defensive linebacker, including the safety, to rip off the quarterback's head. Damn right I don't believe you. If it will make you feel better, I had the cleaning service get the guest room upstairs ready for you."

"You did?"

"Yeah." Looking at her now, all soft and sexy and sleepy, he wanted nothing more than to put her in his bed. Not for anything physical, he wasn't that insensitive a jerk. After all she was pregnant.

He just wanted her here. When he had told her he was tired of sleeping alone, he hadn't realized how true it was until the moment she had said she was going to the guest house. For a split second, he'd thought she was going to say it was herself she was afraid of. And the look in her eyes had almost made him think she wanted him as more than a friend. Then the look was gone, replaced by fear.

He couldn't stand that. As much as he had resisted getting the upstairs room ready, now he was glad he had. He had sworn he would never marry again, but he had. Only because his relationship with Kelly was different. It wasn't love. There was no such thing.

"You don't mind separate rooms?" she asked.

"Nope."

"What happened to all that stuff about being lonely? And your empty bed?"

He waved a hand as if to dismiss her misgivings.

"It was just talk. You wanted ten good reasons why we should get married. It was part of the gag."

"You're sure?"

"I've never lied to you." Until now, he thought.

"Then, yes. The guest room would be fine."

"I'll help you bring your stuff over. At least what you'll need for tonight."

She stood on tiptoe and waited for a second. Then she frowned at him, but there was a twinkle in her eyes. "You want to bring your face down here so I can kiss it?"

With his hands still in his pockets, he bent just far enough for her soft lips to reach his cheek. He hoped she wouldn't notice his quickened breathing, his racing heart. He didn't want to scare her off. And if he gave in to his feelings, he would sweep her into his arms for a repeat of their earlier kiss.

He straightened and winked at her. "Come on, Walker. Let's go get your PJs and toothbrush."

"Like a slumber party," she said.

"Yeah." He groaned inwardly.

A hell of a sleep-over. One that lasted four months, with him in a constant state of need.

Sometime in the middle of the night, Kelly got out of bed and walked downstairs. She couldn't sleep. Strange house, strange bed. Different smells. Disturbing thoughts.

She went into the kitchen and turned on the light beneath the hood over the stove. The rest of the house was dark. Blinking at the bright light as she opened the refrigerator, she pulled out the milk carton, then poured some in a mug. After setting it in the microwave to warm, she leaned her back against the bar and listened to the hum, reminding herself to stop it before the beeping woke Mike.

He was the primary reason for her disturbing thoughts.

Earlier, when she had kissed him, she had sensed his response. Although she couldn't believe he wanted her, especially in her present condition, he was a man. Now he was a *married* man and he had agreed to a platonic relationship. She had some idea what that cost him.

She wasn't stupid; she had a brother. She had been around the block once or twice. In fact, lately she understood the hormone battle a whole lot better. Mike was a red-blooded man. He had needs.

And he had put his physical needs aside for her. He was a real friend. She didn't ever want to lose that.

She wanted to return the favor. But how?

"Something wrong, Kel?"

She whirled around, heart pounding. "Mike!"

"Couldn't you sleep?"

"Where did you come from?"

"There," he said, nodding toward the family room.

With the breakfast bar between them, she could only see him from the waist up. But his naked torso was enough to make her whacked-out hormones purr. Her eyes were drawn to the masculine sprinkling of hair on his chest, wide over the curved muscle below his collar bone, then tapering lower to his flat midsection. She swallowed hard, hoping like crazy that he was wearing something. She really didn't want this to be the second time she saw him naked. Not when she was a swirling, seething swamp of female pheromone. She was here because of one mistake. She didn't want to make another, even bigger, one.

"Why were you on the sofa?" she asked.

"There's rice in our—I mean my bed."

His gaze dropped to a spot just below her chin, then quickly lifted again. She wished she'd thought to put on a robe, but hoped her fleece gown was thick enough. She instinctively hunched her shoulders forward.

Mike pushed splayed fingers through his hair. "And rice isn't all. Come and see what else your friend Susan did."

"How do you know it was her?"

"Remember when she disappeared for so long during the reception?"

"Yes, but—"

"Let me take you into the bedroom and show you her handiwork." He walked to the end of the bar.

Her cheeks burning, Kelly quickly shut her eyes. If he was buck-naked, she didn't want to know.

"I'm wearing boxers, Kel." Amusement filled his voice.

"Thank God." She released her breath and looked at him.

He held out his hand. "Come with me."

She hesitated a second before putting her fingers into his palm. His big warm hand felt good wrapped around hers. If things had been different, she would be sleeping in that downstairs room with him. Before she could stop it, regret and longing rose up inside her. She pushed it away as fast as she could.

He took her down the hall and turned to his left. He flipped a switch, and the lights went on. It took a few seconds for her eyes to adjust.

The master bedroom was big; she had forgotten just how big. There was a California king-sized bed to accommodate Mike's size, an oak armoire across from that and a matching dresser on the other wall. In front of the French doors that led out to the patio and pool and spa beyond, there were two powder blue, wingback chairs with a circular table between. Even with all the furniture, and these were big pieces, there was still a lot of rug to vacuum. And a good sweeping was definitely called for right now.

There was rice all over the hunter green carpet.

"Susan was busy," Kelly said as she took in the far corners of the room. "Looks like the Fourth of July in here."

Red, white and blue crepe paper streamers crisscrossed the ceiling, anchored by something that appeared to be balloons. When she looked closer, she saw that they were condoms, blown up and taped to every corner of the room, hanging from the brass lamps on the dresser and nightstands.

She walked to the bed and looked. There was a ton of rice still on the sheets. Glancing back at Mike's tall, muscular body, she couldn't help noticing that there was just flimsy cotton underwear between her and Mike Cameron in the flesh—bare flesh. She turned back to the bed.

Mike walked up behind her. She could feel the heat of him through her fleece nightgown.

"I'm only surprised she didn't tie bells underneath the mattress," he said.

"Bells? What for?" Kelly frowned. Then she got it and her cheeks burned. "Oh, you mean if we—"

"Yeah." His voice was grim, confirming her earlier misgivings about his sacrifice.

"Mike, I need to talk to you about something."

"Is that why you were up warming milk at this hour of the night? Something's on your mind?"

She nodded. "I just wanted to tell you that if you

want to date, and—'' she nodded toward the bed
"—you know. Well, I'll understand. And I just want
you to know that it's all right with me.''

Chapter Five

Mike couldn't believe he'd heard her right. "What did you say?"

"If you want to date, I understand. It's all right."

"The hell it is. I'm a married man. I don't cheat on my wife."

"It wouldn't be cheating if I said it was okay."

"No matter what you say, it's not okay. It's nuts, Kelly. The ink isn't even dry on our marriage certificate and you're talking divorce and affairs."

She sat down on the edge of the bed and sighed. "You're a normal, red-blooded man. I'm trying to be sensitive."

"I'm shocked that you'd even suggest that I should see other women."

"Why? This is not a traditional union."

"No, but this is a traditional small town, with traditional small-town attitudes and traditional narrow minds. They frown on their teachers having affairs. Of all people, you should know what can happen."

Hurt filled her eyes before she lowered her gaze to her clasped hands. "As you pointed out once, I don't have a belt. But you're developing a bad habit of hitting below it."

"I'm sorry. I don't mean to bring that up again. But you *were* threatened with termination for being pregnant."

"No, for not being married."

"Okay. But what do you think McCutcheon would do if someone spotted me with another woman?"

"You could be discreet."

"The chances of pulling it off—even if I wanted to—are slim to none."

Mike had sown his share of wild oats and thought he'd seen it all, but this... The woman he'd married less than twelve hours ago had calmly told him to date—if the need arose. Even more shocking to him, he couldn't think of a single woman he'd rather be with than the beautiful, pregnant one sitting on his bed. Maybe he *had* been tackled one too many times without a helmet.

Mike sat down beside her and rested his elbows on his knees. "If I was caught in an affair, Doug would have a field day. He'd chew you up and spit you out if he makes good on his threat to push the custody issue. What would that do to your chances of keeping the baby? That's why we did this in the first place. Remember?" he asked sharply.

"I'm trying to think of everyone." She twisted her fingers in her lap. "I'm afraid you'll hate me. I don't want to lose you as my friend, Mike." She bowed her head, and her hair swept forward, hiding her face like a brown silk curtain.

"Have I ever lied to you, Kelly?"

She sniffed. "Not that I can remember."

"It's not my style."

"I thought you said you don't have a style."

"I do when it comes to friendship. I don't lie and I don't keep things from my friends. Trust me. If I need a woman, you'll be the first to know. Okay?"

"Okay." She sniffled.

"Now, shall we go put some chocolate in that warm milk?"

She nodded. "You want some? It's good for what ails you."

"Okay."

Kelly looked at him and smiled. Her beauty burrowed deep inside him and warmed every cold corner of his heart. It zapped him like a lightning bolt. What he felt for Kelly was more than friendship. He didn't dare say that to her, though. If he did, she would be outta there like a wide receiver with the long ball. He'd promised not to lie to her, and he couldn't tell her the truth.

This was something chocolate couldn't fix. Maybe nothing could.

Kelly lay flat on her back on the exam table waiting for the ultrasound technician. She stared at the white sheet over her belly. "I look like a covered wagon."

Mike laughed. "This may or may not be an attempt at humor by exaggeration. Either way, I'm not getting sucked in. No comment," he said, grinning.

Kelly's heart did that little skip it always did when he smiled at her that way. Why was it the bigger she got the better looking he got?

"Chicken," she said with a sniff.

"Smart," he returned. "If I say you don't look like

a covered wagon, you'll say I'm lying or need glasses. If I agree with you, you'll rip out my throat.''

"Have I really been that cranky?" she asked, afraid she'd pushed his good nature to the breaking point. "You didn't have to come with me for this test."

"No, you have not been cranky. And I didn't have to come with you. I wanted to."

School had ended for summer vacation, and she didn't have any responsibilities until September at Stevenson High School. The issue of her termination had been dropped after her marriage, now a month and a half old. She had changed her name from Walker to Cameron on everything from her driver's license and school district personnel file to her medical records. She and Mike had developed a routine in the house and had settled into an easy, comfortable living arrangement. He was supportive, fun and surprisingly tidy for a man. As a roommate, she couldn't ask for more.

As for her feelings, she could ask for less. A lot less. Sharing a house with him was very intimate. She saw Mike first thing in the morning and last thing at night. They did laundry together and were learning an intricate kitchen choreography as they cooked meals side by side. Laughter and good-natured disagreements were a normal part of their day. It was becoming increasingly difficult to ignore the way her heart skipped a beat when he entered a room, the goose bumps his deep voice raised on her arms, her eager anticipation to see him when he was away from the house. These reactions were more than friendship, and slipping dangerously close to "romantic attraction." What if the male-female thing didn't go away after the baby was born?

She sighed. "Oh, go ahead, Mike. Take your best shot at this misshapen body. I'm tough. I can take it."

"You're the English teacher and I'm sure you'll correct me if I'm wrong, but doesn't the prefix *mis* imply bad or wrong?"

"It does."

"Then let me point out there is nothing wrong with the way you look. For a pregnant lady, due to deliver in five weeks—"

"Four," she quickly corrected him.

"Four weeks," he said, without missing a beat, "you look exactly the way you should. Healthy, glowing and very beautiful, I might add."

"Flatterer," she grumbled. "And on the edge of fibber. If this is the way I was meant to look *four* weeks before giving birth, then the term *Mother Nature* should be *Father*, and proof positive that God is indeed a man."

"I notice you've gone from thinking in terms of so many months along to how many weeks until kickoff."

Kelly winced at his euphemism. "That's a very uncomfortable visual."

"Sorry." He shifted, and the chair beside her squeaked. "I'm going to have to keep my mouth shut to avoid putting my foot in it."

"Good idea, Cameron. The next crack you hear could be your head," she said jokingly.

As they laughed, the technician walked in. "Mr. and Mrs. Cameron, my name is Stephanie Daniels. Are you ready to get started?"

"Yes," Kelly answered.

"All right. I'm going to turn out the light so there's no glare on the screen. I'll be taking pictures, too, but we don't want the light to obstruct your view of your baby," she said looking directly at Mike.

Interesting, Kelly thought. The technician assumed Mike was the father. It made her pause, but she decided it was easier not to make the correction.

The room went dark, and the only illumination came from the ultrasound machine when it was turned on. Glancing at Mike, Kelly could see his face clearly in the glow.

"The hum you hear is just the fan on the instrument," the technician explained. She picked up a tube and said, "This will be cold."

After the squirt, Kelly felt the gel on her abdomen. "Yikes," she gasped, sucking in her breath.

"You okay?" Mike said, taking her hand.

"Fine. Cold doesn't completely describe that stuff. Do you keep it in the freezer?"

Stephanie laughed. "Now I'm going to press the probe against you. It won't hurt, just a firm pressure. I need to find the optimum position." She concentrated on her job.

With her abdomen partially exposed, Kelly was glad the lights were out. But when she glanced at Mike, she found he wasn't looking at her. He studied the screen with a look of intense fascination on his face. "That's a real live little person in there."

"You didn't think I looked like this for nothing, did you?"

"No, but— I guess one picture is worth a thousand words. Wow!"

Stephanie moved the probe, and when she did, there was a click as she took a picture of the baby's position. She explained that the fetus was normal in size for the number of weeks of gestation. Heart looked fine, internal organs in an appropriate stage of development, hands and feet as they should be.

She looked at several more views, then glanced at Kelly and Mike. "Would you like to know the sex of your baby?"

"No," Mike said.

"Yes," Kelly answered at the same time. She shrugged. "I'd like to know whether to buy blue or pink."

Mike squeezed her hand that he still held in his. "It's your ball game."

Kelly looked at the other woman. "We'd like to know the baby's sex."

"You understand this isn't one hundred percent accurate. And the position of the infant isn't ideal for prediction. Don't hold me to this—"

"I understand. Your best guess. Boy or girl?" Kelly held her breath.

"Boy."

Kelly's heart jumped. A boy. She wasn't even sure why, but that was exactly what she'd hoped to hear. She looked at Mike for a reaction. He frowned for a second, then met her gaze.

"Is something wrong?" she asked.

"No." He slowly shook his head.

"What is it? I know you, Cameron. There's something going on. Spill it."

One dark eyebrow lifted, and he smiled a little sheepishly. "I sort of wanted to see a little girl who looked just like you."

Kelly's eyes filled with tears. "That's the sweetest thing you've ever said to me."

"I'm not trying to be sweet. I only do that when you

compare yourself to a covered wagon." He rubbed his thumb across her knuckles.

Stephanie smiled indulgently. "If I were you, I'd keep him around."

Kelly didn't answer. She didn't know what to say. She couldn't keep him. If she did, she would lose the best part of what they had together. Friendship.

A lump formed in her throat. She hadn't counted on these feelings when she'd proposed to Mike. She sighed. At least something was going right, since they'd had no further word from Doug. She put a protective hand on her abdomen. Maybe he had decided "it" wasn't worth the aggravation. She fervently hoped so. She would never let him near this child.

If all went well, when her little boy made his entrance into the world, his mother and his "Uncle Mike" would quietly separate. There would be no emotional trauma to the baby, who would be too young to know what was happening. She could preserve the good thing she and Mike had going. It would all go according to plan.

"Just four more weeks," she whispered.

Mike drove down Lyons Avenue and turned the Bronco right onto Peachland Drive. He glanced at Kelly sitting beside him. She stared out the window at the passing scenery. How could she be so calm? She was carrying a tiny human being inside her. What an enormous responsibility.

"Is the air-conditioning too cold?" he asked, adjusting the control down.

"No, it's fine."

"Do you feel all right? You look tired."

She shrugged. "No more than usual."

"The doctor said the baby's fully formed now and will just put on weight during the last weeks. Are you eating enough?"

She glanced ruefully at her abdomen then back at him. "Yeah. I think so."

"But the doctor said—"

"Mike, what's wrong with you? The doctor and the ultrasound tech said the baby is fine. Why are we playing twenty questions about my health?"

He shook his head, thinking. How could he put into words what he was feeling? "I guess it just hit me."

She smiled softly. "That there's really a baby in here knocking on the walls to get out?"

"Yeah."

"But you've felt him move. That was real."

"Those little ripples were—"

"You call those little ripples?" She stared at him in mock outrage. "When this character decides to flex his muscles, it feels more like a 6.0 on the Richter scale."

"That's good. Right? Means he's strong and healthy?"

She folded her hands over her belly and studied him, a little surprised. "This is a Mike Cameron I've never seen before. Who'd have thought an ultrasound would be a religious experience for you?"

"Go ahead. Make fun. But this is the first time I've ever been through anything like that. And it was pretty—" He searched for the right word, and the only one he could come up with was "Awesome."

She shifted in her seat, adjusting her shoulder belt more comfortably. "You know I love to tease you every chance I get, but I can't do it this time. I felt the same way the first time I saw the baby."

"He was real to you from the first, though. Wasn't he?"

"Yes. How did you know?"

"Because there was another alternative that would have been a hell of a lot easier for you. You didn't have to have him."

Her expression turned serious. "You're wrong about that. I did have to. For me it was the only choice."

He drove up the driveway and stopped in front of the house. When he turned off the ignition, he slanted his upper body toward her. "You're quite a woman, Kel."

"No, I'm not—"

"Just sit tight and let me pay you a compliment. I admire the hell out of you. I got a sneak peek at what you're in for. That baby is going to be a big job. Feedings, changing diapers, trying to figure out what he needs because he can't tell you. You were going to do that by yourself—"

"I still am."

"But I'm—"

"You're my friend. The best I've ever had. To keep it that way, I'm moving out the beginning of September, just before school starts. I still plan to raise the baby alone."

Mike gripped the steering wheel, not quite sure what he was feeling, although anger was right there at the top of his list. She did nothing more than remind him of their original agreement. It had been his idea.

But something had shifted for him today. He wasn't so sure he wanted to let that bargain stand. He almost blurted it out, but the wary expression on her face stopped him. She didn't want to hear; he didn't want to upset her.

He took a deep breath, putting aside what he'd been about to say. "You won't mind some company from time to time, will you?"

"Of course not. I'm sure little Sam will look forward to lots of visits with you."

"You're naming him Sam?"

She nodded. "It's a strong name. And I want him to be strong like his Uncle Mike."

He blinked, wondering where that had come from. She was really keeping arm's distance from him. What was this "Uncle Mike" baloney?

As she struggled to remove her seat belt, he reached over and released it. Now wasn't the time to confront her about this. He had seen for himself how intimately her welfare and the baby's were connected. He wouldn't do anything to chance harming either of them. He would keep his cool and wait for a good time. But whenever or wherever that would be, one thing he knew for sure...

A showdown was coming.

Kelly stared at the small trivia game card in her hand and silently read the science question. It was an easy one and would give Mike the last little pie-shaped piece to fill in his wheel. Again. He was far too insufferable when he won. She would go to almost any lengths to keep that from happening.

She looked at him without blinking. "What's the atomic weight of Denver?"

His eyebrows drew together in a puzzled frown. Then he noticed the grin she couldn't hide and pointed an accusing finger at her. "You made that up."

She held up her hand and put the other palm over her heart. "As God is my witness..."

"Stuff a sock in it, Kel. Let me see that card."

She put it behind her back. "You'll look at the answer."

"The answer is not in question here. The question is in question."

"Why?" she innocently asked.

"It's a stupid question. If it was on the up-and-up, you'd hand over that card."

"Aren't you getting tired of this game?" she asked. "We've been at it for hours."

Since right after dinner. Mike had come home from summer football practice, showered and helped her with dinner and the dishes. She'd suggested the game. It was scraping the bottom of the excuse barrel, looking for ways to take her far-too-active imagination off Mike.

He sat on the floor across from her with the oak coffee table and game board between them. His grin was enough to make her pulse do the Charleston. She figured asking him to put a paper bag over his head would generate a conversation that she didn't want to have, so she discarded the idea.

The problem with this trivia contest was that it was a classic example of why she and Mike were such close friends. He was good at answering science, geography and sports questions. Kelly knew history, literature and entertainment stuff. They demolished the competition when they played partners. If it was just the two of them, the game dragged on forever. Kelly had the uncomfortable feeling that they were two halves of the same wheel, and she needed Mike to keep her rolling.

She couldn't remember a time when he hadn't been her friend. If everything went as she hoped, that wouldn't change.

The doorbell rang. "I'll get it," Kelly said, standing and stretching with the game card still in her hand. "I need to move around."

She seized the opportunity to postpone asking Mike Who invented the railroad sleeping car in 1859? What kind of a science question was that? Any idiot could figure out that it was Mr. Pullman. Mike wouldn't know the "George M." part, so she might be able to get him on a technicality. After she got rid of whoever was at the front door.

"Don't you want to leave that here?" he asked, pointing to the question card in her hand.

"Not on your life, Cameron. You cheat."

"Me? The question you just gave me is as phony as a three-dollar bill. You've got a nerve—"

Ignoring his good-natured tirade, she walked to the front of the house. The entryway wood was cool against her bare feet. Through the glass in the door, she could see the silhouette of a woman.

Kelly opened the door. "Yes?"

The attractive blonde in jeans held a manila envelope in her hands. "Are you Kelly Walker Cameron?"

"That's right."

"This is for you. Will you please sign for it?"

Kelly took the packet and put her signature on the attached slip, which the woman promptly removed. "Have a nice day, Mrs. Cameron."

"Thank you." What in the world could this be? she wondered.

Kelly shut the door and turned the envelope over. In the upper left hand corner was the return address. The names Burns, Banks, Boyle and Smith, Attorneys at Law, caused a knot to tighten in her chest. She ripped open the flap, pulled out the pristine white papers, then read the top left corner.

Doug had made good on his threat.

"Kelly? Who's at the door?" Mike called from the other room.

She couldn't answer. Fear and rage lumped in her throat closing it off.

"Kelly?"

The next moment Mike was beside her. "What is it, Kel? You're white as a sheet."

When she held out the papers to him, her hand was shaking.

Mike read through them quickly. "He's suing you for custody of the baby?"

"Damn him. He won't get away with this. I'll fight him with everything I've got." She looked at Mike. "What have I got?"

"I told you what the lawyer said. His advice then was to do nothing. Wait and see. He figured Hammond was bluffing."

"He figured wrong," Kelly said, slanting a glance at the papers still in his hand. "Now I need to do something—and fast."

Her stomach started churning, and she was afraid she might lose her lunch, something she hadn't done since the beginning of her pregnancy. Now that she was nearing the end of it, she couldn't bear the idea that she might lose custody of her baby. The thought of a jerk like Doug raising him was intolerable.

An intense pain tightened across her abdomen. Kelly gasped and doubled over.

"What's wrong, Kel?" Mike asked sharply. He put his arm around her.

She sucked air in through her teeth. "I—I don't know."

"Is the baby coming?"

"Too early," she said on a gasp of breath.

"Can you walk?"

The pain lessened and she straightened. "Yes."

He guided her to the family room and sat her down on the sofa. Then he fluffed the pillow behind her back and gently lifted her ankles, swiveling her so that her legs were up and she lay semi-reclined. He pushed the game board out of the way and sat on the table beside her, his face creased with worry.

Her abdomen tightened again and she gritted her teeth. "Here comes another one."

"Are these contractions? Should we start timing them, like they said in Lamaze class? What can I do?" he asked, a desperate note in his voice.

For the second time in the last ten minutes, Kelly was afraid for her baby.

It was too early.

She knew he was fully developed, but his little body needed the next few weeks to mature so he would have an easier time of it when he came into the world.

Before she could control it, tears filled her eyes until everything in front of her wavered, as if she was looking through a rain-slicked window. She blinked hard. "If something happens to the baby—" Her voice cracked and she stopped.

"He'll be fine, Kelly." Mike lifted her hand and placed it between his own. "Take deep breaths," he said.

"What if this is labor? What if Sam comes too early? What if there's something wrong—"

"It's not labor," he said firmly. "It's stress. Damn

that two-bit shyster—'' He clamped his mouth shut, and it was several moments before he spoke again. ''Nothing's going to happen, because you're going to calm down.''

''How can I? Doug is planning to take my baby. I don't know how to stop him.''

''Let me handle that weasel. You just think about yourself and the baby. I plan to beat him at his own game—''

''It's a lawsuit, Mike. That *is* his game.'' Although panic was very close to the surface, it had been a few minutes since the last pain. She was feeling a little better. Maybe Mike was right and this was just a reaction to the shock of learning that Doug was serious. If anyone had told her that the lesser of two evils would be facing off with Doug Hammond for her baby's custody, she wouldn't have believed it.

''Lawsuits are filed all the time. This one isn't worth the time and energy it would take to blow it to hell,'' Mike said. ''You're working yourself up over a piece of paper.''

''If I thought for one minute that he sincerely cared, it wouldn't be so bad. But he's only interested in being a father if it will further his career. What will happen to Sam if Doug wins?''

Another sharp pain gripped her, and she squeezed Mike's fingers.

''Another one?'' he asked, tightening his hold on her hand.

She nodded. ''It's not as bad, though.''

''Kelly, you've got to relax.''

''I can't. Not until I know Doug won't get his hands on my baby.''

"Trust me, Kel. I'm telling you he will never take this child from you."

"How can you know that?"

"Because I'll handle Doug." His voice was hard as granite.

Kelly saw the fierce expression in his dark eyes, and it frightened her. Not because she knew him and how much he wanted to use the Neanderthal approach. What scared her more was how much she wished she *could* let him take over and deal with Doug. But if she did, they would cross the line into territory that might alter their friendship. She didn't think she could get through this without Mike. Not just because he was her friend, but because she needed a man, or more specifically a husband. She had to look more stable if they went to court in a custody battle.

She felt guilty for using Mike, then reminded herself that the marriage idea had been his in the first place. But that didn't give him the right to take over.

She pulled her hands from his grasp. "If you'll give me the number of your attorney, I'll call him and take care of this."

Mike shook his head. "Absolutely not."

"Why?"

This was not the way their friendship had always worked. He was trying to shut her out.

"You're in no shape to call him. You're too emotional."

So, things between them were already changing. Friends talked to each other and faced problems together.

Some choice. She could take full responsibility of the situation, walk out on their agreement and risk losing her baby. Or let Mike run the show and lose the best friend she'd ever had.

Maybe there was one other thing she could do. If Mike called her bluff, she knew she would have to eat crow and stay with him for her baby's sake. But it was worth a try.

She sat up and swung her legs over the side of the couch. "Then our agreement is over, Mike."

Chapter Six

Mike stared at her for a second. "Why?"

She met his gaze squarely. "We agreed to marry for a lot of reasons. The most important was to present a united front should Doug make good on his threat. He's done that, but you're welshing on your promise."

"How do you figure?"

"Excuse me, but the word *united* implies more than one person. It's damn hard to unite by yourself. And that's what you're doing by leaving me out of the legal part of this."

"I'm trying to protect you, Kelly."

"I don't need you to do that. I took care of myself before we got married—"

"And a fine job you've done of it—" He ran a hand through his hair, then looked at her. "I'm sorry."

"Forget it. You're absolutely right. I made mistakes, but they're mine and I'll take care of them. I'll continue to do so after this marriage is over."

"What are you saying?"

"I'm moving back into the guest house. If it's all right with you I'll stay there until the baby's born. As soon as I can, I'll find a place for us to live."

"You're in no condition to be by yourself. That's dumber than your fake trivia question."

"I already owe you more than I can ever repay. You married me, gave my baby a name and saved my job. For some reason being my husband has made you think you can change the rules. I won't let you do that and jeopardize our friendship. We're married, yes. But the decisions are mine."

Mike studied her. She looked beautiful, fragile. Desperation darkened her green eyes. But beneath it all, he sensed her determination. She was the strongest woman he knew. She reminded him that she would be fine when they ended the marriage. But he didn't want her to go. There was no doubt in his mind that she would if he didn't back off. He couldn't think about tomorrow right now. He just knew he couldn't picture today without Kelly in it.

"You win, Kel. I'll give you his card. It's in my file."

"Thank you, Mike. May I have it now, please?"

"Sure. It's upstairs in my desk. I'll make a deal with you. You put up your feet, and I'll go get it." He held out his hand.

"Thanks, Mike," she said placing her fingers in his palm.

A pretty pink color flushed her cheeks, and he knew she was remembering the last time they had sealed an agreement on this very sofa. He had kissed her. He wanted to do the same thing now, but he was afraid it would be more than a friendly touch on the lips. Then she would accuse him of changing the rules again, and she would be out of there as fast as she could go.

Mike climbed the stairs, frustration gnawing at him. He wanted to take Hammond apart. He could think of very few things in life that would give him more satisfaction. But he couldn't. For Kelly's sake. She would worry about the consequences to himself, possible legal action and how it might affect his reputation and job.

For some reason she thought she was an inconvenience to him. Obviously it was important for her to do this on her own. He wished he could convince her that he liked having her in his life. He wanted to be in hers. And that was far more important than any minor irritation Doug Hammond might cause.

But he was concerned about her and the baby and what all that stress would do to her if he argued with her. Protecting her was uppermost in his mind. That put him between a rock and a hard place. He was afraid that an ugly custody battle would take a toll on her, while he just stood by and watched. But if he ran interference, she would leave him before their agreement was up.

Mike pulled the business card holder from the upper right hand drawer in his desk. Tim Sargent's card was on the first page in the plastic pocket. He looked at it, and an idea began to form. Maybe there was a way for him to protect her after all.

He dialed his friend's office number and the receptionist answered. "Sargent, McCarthy and Harrison," she said.

"Tina? Mike Cameron."

"Hi, Mr. C. How the heck are you? Long time no see."

"I'm fine. Is Tim in the office this afternoon?"

His tone must have told her his business was serious, because her manner changed instantly. "Yes, sir. I'll put you right through."

In seconds, Mike heard his friend's voice. "Hi, Mike. What's up?"

Kelly called from downstairs, "What's taking so long, Mike?"

"Hold on, Tim." He put his hand over the receiver and shouted, "I'm having trouble finding the card. I know it's here somewhere. Just sit tight." He spoke into the phone again. "I don't have time for a long explanation, Tim. Just listen."

"Shoot, buddy."

"Remember the woman I told you about who might have a child custody battle on her hands?"

"The pregnant one?"

"Yeah. The father filed suit. She's going to call you. Talk to her. Reassure her. This part is critical, don't tell her anything that will upset her. I'll call you later to discuss the case. I want everything to go through me. Is that clear?"

"As mud," Tim said.

"You're a silver-tongued devil. You can handle it."

"Will do."

"Thanks, Tim. I owe you one." Mike hung up the phone, then wrote the number on a piece of paper for Kelly.

He'd sunk pretty low this time, he thought. But didn't the end justify the means? In the end Kelly and the baby would be safe, and that was all he cared about.

He didn't want to think about what she would do if she found out about this. With luck she never would.

Kelly savored the warm, secure touch of Mike's hand at the small of her back as he ushered her through the coffee shop to a secluded table. They had just completed the series of classes preparing for the baby's birth, and he had suggested they celebrate with a hot-fudge sundae. In approximately two weeks, she would find out if the breathing technique worked. She wanted very much to have natural childbirth, without drugs to harm the baby. But after seeing the birthing films tonight, she wasn't so sure she had what it took.

When they stopped at the booth, Kelly eyeballed the space for her belly between the stationary table and the tufted cushion back. One corner of her mouth lifted as she looked at Mike. "I don't think I'll fit."

He grabbed a chair from an empty table and placed it on the end for her. "There."

"Thanks," she said, sitting down.

He slid into the space beside her. A waitress took their orders. When she was gone, Mike rested his forearm on the table and brushed against hers. The touch sent tingles sparking up her arm. Wasn't that just dandy? She was as big as a battleship, so enormous she couldn't fit into a booth, and more aware than ever of his masculinity. When his gaze met hers, she would have sworn he felt it, too.

"Why are you looking at me that way?" he asked.

She squirmed on her chair. "What way?"

Oh, Lord, did he know what she was thinking? Could he see that she was attracted to him? She thought she'd been doing such a good job of hiding it.

"You just look funny. Are you all right? Go ahead, spill your guts," he coaxed.

"Interesting way of phrasing things after what we saw tonight."

"You're scared, aren't you?"

"Yes," she said.

But not only for the reasons he was talking about. She was afraid he would see what she was beginning to understand. Her feelings for Mike were not just appreciation of a good-looking man. They weren't even just hormonal. She was scared that she might be falling for Mike.

Still, with her choices of trying to ignore what he did to her or being alone, she would take the former. Tonight's class had forced her to see that the only way out of her present condition was going through the actual birth. She *was* scared of the unknown. Afraid that she couldn't handle the pain, that she would let herself, her baby and Mike down.

She was glad he had agreed to be her coach and would be there with her. He was the best coach in the whole world—even off the football field.

"You're going to do fine, Kel. You were the best student in Lamaze class. This birth thing will be a piece of cake."

"I sure hope so. I wish my mom could be here."

His mouth pulled into a straight line, and sympathy filled his eyes as he lifted her hand and placed it between his own. "You're not alone. I'll be there."

"Thanks, Mike."

If only she had the words to tell him how grateful she was for that. And for him backing off and letting her talk to the attorney about Doug's lawsuit. It had bothered her that he'd tried to leave her out of the decision-making process. She had every right to be part of the fight. She did wonder how the fight was going. There hadn't been any word from the attorney since her initial phone call.

She looked at Mike. "I haven't heard from Tim Sargent. Do you think that's a good sign?"

He was drinking water and started to cough after her question. She pounded him on the back. "Are you all right?"

He nodded. "Went down the wrong way."

"So do you think no news is good news? With the custody suit, I mean."

"I'd say good news," he said.

"That's what I think, too. He told me not to worry."

The waitress brought their hot-fudge sundaes and set one down in front of each of them.

Mike picked up his spoon. "Then I'd say don't worry. He's the expert."

"But it seems like there should have been *some* news by now. Tim talked about countersuits and possible criminal charges. He was vague, and I didn't understand it all, but when I pressed him he said when he had formulated a plan of attack, he would let me know."

"Then I think you should stop worrying until the need arises. If it ever does."

"It's been three weeks, Mike. Are you sure he's competent? It seems to be taking him a long time to figure out what to do. I'm no authority on the subject, but I'd say if he planned the invasion of Europe during World War II, we might all be speaking German now."

"You're exaggerating, Kel. He's got to figure out how to circumvent Doug, check case law—"

"There can't be that many cases where a father sues the pregnant mother for custody?"

"I've known Tim since college. He's one of the brightest guys I know. If brains don't work, he can fight down-and-dirty. Don't worry. Doug is not going to get little Sam there," he said, pointing his spoon at her abdomen.

Kelly realized she hadn't taken a bite of her ice cream yet and found she wasn't as hungry as she'd thought. She made an attempt, but finally Mike finished hers.

"You look tired. Ready to go home?"

She nodded. "My back aches. Home sounds heavenly."

Sometime around two-thirty in the morning, a nagging pain in her back made Kelly sit up in bed wide awake. As she rubbed the area, the discomfort spread, tightening like a steel band around her abdomen. It didn't last long, and excitement along with fear swelled inside her when she wondered if this was labor.

"If this is it," she said to herself, "that wasn't too bad. Maybe I can do this after all."

She swung her legs over the side of the bed and clicked on the light beside her. Noting the time, she waited. Five minutes later she had another pain. During her last doctor's appointment she had fortunately thought to ask at what point she should go to the hospital. "The doctor said when they're five minutes apart. Do I wait for another one and time it? Is one enough? Oh, God, I don't know what to do."

Mike will know, she thought. She put on a robe and went downstairs, stopping outside his bedroom door. She knocked softly. "Mike?"

There was no answer. She knocked again and opened the door. "Mike, wake up."

The ceiling fan hummed overhead and threw a breeze that chilled her damp skin. She shivered, and

Kelly wasn't sure if it was from cold or fear. "Mike, please wake up," she said louder this time.

The figure in the bed moved as he rolled toward her. In the silver moonlight peeking through the curtains, she could see that his dark hair was rumpled from sleep. This time she didn't care if he was naked, she needed him and she was so thankful he was there.

"Kelly? What's wrong? Is it the baby?"

"I'm not sure."

He sat up and turned on the light. Patting the mattress beside him he said, "Come on in. We'll wait this out together."

She walked around the bed and crawled in beside him, resting against the pillow he fluffed for her. "I'm sorry to wake you. I'm just not sure. It's a little early, but I had a pain in my back. Then five minutes later there was another one."

"How long since the last pain?" he asked.

Mike put his arm around her and pulled her against his side. His skin was warm and his body solid and comforting.

She glanced at the red digital numbers on his nightstand clock. "Five minutes."

"Don't we need to go to the hospital?" he asked, his voice sharp.

"What if they stop? It's still a couple weeks until my due date."

"What if they don't stop? You don't want to wait too long." He threw the sheet aside and started to get up.

Kelly stopped him with a hand on his forearm. "Wait, Mike. Give me a minute."

His gaze darted over her face and his expression softened. "Don't be scared, Kel."

"I'm trying not to be." The feel of his strong arm beneath her fingers comforted her. She knew Mike would take care of her. "We're friends. Right?"

"The best. But this is a hell of a time to discuss that—"

"You know I'd do anything for you. You'd do anything for me. Right?"

"Yeah, Kel." She knew he was agitated when he ran his fingers through his hair for a second time. He needed a shave, and the stubble shadow gave him a dark, dangerous look. "I don't know where you're going with this, but make it fast, honey."

"I think you should go through labor for me."

"If I could, believe me I would." His look said he meant every word. "I wish there was something I could say to put you at ease."

"You're a coach, Mike. What would you tell your players if they were in a championship game and so nervous they thought they might throw up?"

"I'd tell them they were a well-oiled machine. They were trained for it." One corner of his mouth lifted in a grin. "Come to think of it, that's not bad advice for you."

"The well-oiled machine part?"

"The training part."

"I can't seem to remember the instruction—" She stopped as a pain knotted in her lower back, then squeezed around her belly.

"Breathe, Kel. Remember?"

When he demonstrated, Kelly followed his lead and everything came back to her. When it was over, she said, "That one was longer. A little more intense."

"That does it. I'm taking you to the hospital."

"But—"

"But nothing. If it's a false alarm, it won't do any harm. They'll send us home and we'll get some sleep. Otherwise we'll be up all night wondering."

Kelly sighed. "You're right. They're professionals. It *would* make me feel better to be where they know what they're doing."

He glanced at her and one dark eyebrow raised. "What am I? Chopped liver?"

"When's the last time you delivered a baby?"

"You've got a point. I don't want to play catch, either. Get a move on. Is your bag packed?"

She nodded. "It's by the door in my room."

He dressed quickly in jeans and a T-shirt. "I'll get it. Relax and don't worry."

As he disappeared upstairs, Kelly had another contraction. Definitely show time.

"Kel?"

Mike looked down at her in the hospital bed. The sheet that covered her stomach was flat. No more covered wagon. He grinned.

She opened her eyes and smiled back at him. "Hi, Coach."

"Hi, little mother. You did good. How do you feel?" he asked, sitting beside her on the bed. The curtain suspended from chains and surrounding her bed gave them relative privacy.

"How do I feel? I'm an English teacher for goodness' sake and I have no words to describe what I'm feeling. Wonderful. Relieved. Ecstatic. Flabbergasted."

"You could have knocked me over with a feather when the doctor told me we had a girl."

"Dr. Arguile showed a lot of restraint when she didn't deck you after your remark."

"The adrenaline was flowing. With all the excitement, I wasn't thinking clearly."

"I understand. But it was just a little condescending to ask a female doctor if she was sure about the baby's sex. As if all those years of medical school were wasted on a woman."

"I'd have said the same thing if she was a man. Besides, I apologized. She seemed to understand. It had nothing to do with her. I just didn't expect a girl."

"Are you disappointed?"

"Good God, no. I'm the one who was hoping for a miniature of her mother. Remember?"

Kelly's cheeks flushed a nice shade of pink, and her gaze slid away from his as if she was uncomfortable with the remark. But it was true. He had wanted to see a little girl who was the spitting image of Kelly.

Disappointed? Not by a long shot. How could anyone be let down after going through the miracle of birth? A baby with ten fingers and ten toes and a pair of lungs that let her cry loud enough to shatter windows was about the best thing he could imagine. Between that and the fact that her mother was doing just fine, Mike felt like he was on top of the world.

He studied his wife and his heart skipped a beat. He'd seen her dressed to kill for her high school prom. At his last New Year's Eve party, her sexy little black dress and matching high-heeled shoes had gotten the big-time attention of every red-blooded male there. Including him.

But right at this moment, without makeup, her hair pushed back off her face, in a hospital gown, she was the most beautiful woman he had ever seen. She was really something special; she had more guts than anyone he could think of. He'd seen firsthand the pain she'd gone through, and he admired the hell out of her for choosing to have this baby. She'd almost lost her composure a time or two, but she'd hung in there. Once she'd squeezed his hand so hard he wondered if he would lose the feeling in his fingers. Four and a half hours from start to finish and there was a brand new six-and-a-half-pound baby girl to show for it. Not a bad night's work.

Kelly smoothed her hand over her flat abdomen and sighed with what he could only think of as pure pleasure. "I have my body back."

"You make it sound as if you were possessed."

Her forehead puckered thoughtfully. "In a way I guess I was."

"You're not disappointed, that she's a girl I mean? You said you wanted a boy."

"I'm not upset in the least," she said, then looked a little anxious. "She's perfect. Right? I saw you checking her out."

"You checked her out yourself, right after they handed her to you." He smiled and took her hand, cradling it between his own. "But for the record she's the most beautiful baby I have ever seen."

"Out of how many newborns?"

He shifted his weight on the mattress. "I haven't exactly seen that many. Or any, to be exact. But I know quality when I see it," he said, looking into her huge green eyes.

She was quietly thoughtful for a few moments. Just when he was about to ask her if something was bothering her, she said, "I've been thinking about names."

"Yeah. You've been calling her Sam. She kind of threw you a curve."

"I still like the name Sam. How does Samantha

Michele sound to you?'' She looked at him doubtfully, as if she thought he might not approve.

"Would I be jumping to conclusions if I assumed that the Michele part was after me?''

"Would you consider it an honor?''

"Oh, yeah,'' he said. "The best.''

Kelly's smile was so radiant his breath caught.

"I'm glad you think so,'' she said. "You were wonderful, Mike. I don't think I could have done it without you. When Sammi's old enough to understand, I plan to tell her all about how her Uncle Mike helped deliver her.''

There was that Uncle Mike stuff again. He knew she was reminding him that their marriage had a beginning, a middle and now the end was in sight. At the thought, disappointment hit him. Kelly had knocked the wind out of him just as surely as if he'd been tackled without warning.

It was for the best that he remember their time together was coming to an end. He had done the relationship game once, and he wasn't very good at it. Probably because he didn't believe true love existed. His mood turned suddenly bittersweet.

Now he would have two ladies to miss when he and Kelly ended their marriage.

Chapter Seven

Kelly had looked forward to taking care of her baby at home, since finding out she was pregnant. But in that fantasy she had always pictured herself in Mike's guest house, not his king-sized bed. Or rather sitting on his bed. And in her dreams the baby had always slept like an angel. She was not fussy and squirmy, with a red, scrunchy face.

Shifting to a more comfortable sitting position on the mattress, Kelly raised Sammi to her shoulder to burp her. In spite of the reality check, that small, sweet, warm body snuggled in her arms was achingly special. Not to mention frightening. Kelly was responsible for this tiny human being. Sammi couldn't tell her what was wrong when she cried. Kelly was supposed to figure it out. The idea terrified her. Her vision of motherhood had never included mind-numbing terror.

As the panic welled up inside her, Kelly reminded herself that they had just left the hospital that morning. It was close to eight in the evening. They hadn't even been home a whole day. Adjusting would take time. But she was so tired and wished the baby was securely settled so that she could sleep.

Sammi cried loudly in her ear, and Kelly couldn't stop the hot tears that pushed against her eyes. She heard the water in the shower go off and knew Mike would be out soon.

"Thank God," she said.

Her fantasy motherhood had never included Mike, but now she couldn't figure out why it hadn't. He had been there for every major event in her life, including her baby's birth. The bond she shared with him was truly special and one she would safeguard jealously.

Several moments later he appeared in the doorway, drying his damp, dark hair with a towel. The muscles in his arms and shoulders bunched and released with the movement. For several seconds, Kelly stopped breathing as the sight of him mesmerized her. Droplets of water in the hair on his wide chest caught the light and sparkled. If that wasn't enough, the man had the nerve to wear shorts that showed off powerful thighs and calves with a masculine dusting of hair.

He could at least have some consideration for the confused state of her hormones. Any hopes she'd had of getting back to normal right after giving birth were smashed to smithereens with one look at Mike Cameron.

"Everything all right?" he asked.

She tried to speak and found she had to clear her throat. "Everything's fine," she finally managed to say.

"I heard crying. Is something wrong with Little Bit? I thought she was asleep."

Kelly drew in a deep shuddering breath. "I thought

so, too. She seemed sound asleep, then right after you got in the shower, she started crying again. I don't know what's wrong—'' Her voice caught on a sob.

With her arms full of a squealing, wiggling Sammi, Kelly lifted her chin toward the bassinet, trimmed in pink ribbon, which stood between Mike's dresser and the bed. It had been Mike's idea to use the bassinet for naps in his room downstairs during the day rather than the full-size crib upstairs.

She swallowed the lump of emotion and said, "I put her in her crib in my room, and she started to cry."

He sat down beside her on the bed. His shoulder brushed hers, and a quiver of awareness cut through Kelly. The heat of his body burned through her T-shirt, and something smooth and hot spread through her in waves. She was wearing shorts and cursed the vanity that had compelled her to put them on. She had wanted to savor the slimness of her body again. All she had succeeded in doing was exposing more of her skin to the touch of his. That caused her stomach to do back flips.

He braced a hand behind her, breathtakingly near her rear end, and reached across to stroke Sammi's cheek. One of his hands was nearly as big as the baby's back. His strength was obvious and undeniable, making his gentleness with her so touching it formed a lump in Kelly's throat.

"Do you really think something's wrong with her?" he asked, concern furrowing his forehead. "She's fed and her diaper's changed. Right?"

Kelly nodded. "The pediatrician checked her over before we left the hospital and said she's normal and healthy. He warned me that she would be cranky at times and not to worry."

The knot of tension across Kelly's shoulders eased a little, and she knew it was just from voicing her concerns to Mike. An instant of wistfulness flashed through her. If only they were a real family, Sammi's homecoming would be perfect.

Kelly lifted her gaze to Mike's and a sense of longing swept over her, so strong it became a pain in her chest. This was only pretend, she reminded herself. Taking a deep breath, she shifted the crying baby in her arms.

"Have you tried the pacifier?" he asked.

The pacifier! If Kelly hadn't had her arms full of infant she would have slapped her forehead. "I forgot about that little sucker." She giggled at her play on words as a tiny bubble of panic-tinged relief welled up in her.

Mike looked at her a little strangely as he stood up. "I'll get it," he said. "It's in the bassinet."

He lifted the pink plastic plug—how she hated that term—although at the moment she understood and welcomed the blessed little thing. Then he brought it over and gave it to the baby who latched on to it eagerly and made small smacking noises.

"God bless modern technology," Kelly said gratefully. "Some mother I am."

He sat down beside her. "What does that mean?"

"I don't even know what to do when my baby cries."

"Don't be so hard on yourself. You've never done this before."

"Seems a shame, doesn't it? Too bad every baby couldn't be a second child. Not a practice run. Kind of a scary thought that the world is filled with firstborns whose mothers didn't have a clue what they were doing. How messed up do you suppose those people are?''

''Your brother is firstborn. How messed up is he?''

Jim seemed okay. ''You have a point. Still, I can't help wishing now that I'd taken a parenting class.''

''That's no substitute for OJT.''

''Odd jinxed teacher?'' she guessed.

''On the job training,'' he answered, grinning. ''The key is to relax and go through the checklist. She's been fed and diapered. Does she feel warm to you?''

''Oh, God. Do you think she has a fever? Maybe she's not warm enough. In this heat wave, I thought a diaper and undershirt was enough. The doctor said not to put too many clothes on her. Dress her like I would myself. I'm comfortable in shorts—''

His gaze dropped to her legs and a spark of male interest glowed for a moment in his eyes. Then he looked at her. ''Don't borrow trouble, Kelly. It's just on the checklist.'' He leaned over and pressed his lips to Sammi's forehead. ''She feels cool to me.''

''That wasn't very scientific.''

''No, but it works,'' he said. ''She's probably overtired and has gas.''

''What if it's not that simple? What if she keeps crying and needs to see the doctor? What if I wait too long and something really serious happens? What if—''

The baby spit out the pacifier and started to wail again.

Kelly looked at Mike. ''Maybe I should call the doctor?''

''Give her to me, Kelly.''

Her eyebrows shot up. ''What?''

''I said, give her here. Let me hold her for a while.''

Kelly's eyes widened as he took the child out of her arms. He seemed relaxed and in control. "For God's sake, Mike. You're a football coach. What do you know about babies?"

"She's not much different than a football. What's to know?"

"Mike—"

"I'm joking." He took the cloth diaper and placed it over his shoulder, then lifted Sammi up. "I know she's a person, only small. My football players use up a lot of energy. When they're finished, they're tired. All she does is lie around all day. This crying is just her exercise. Like running drills."

She stared at him for a moment. "What scares me the most is that you just made sense."

He grinned, and her heart skipped. "You need a few minutes to yourself."

"To do what? Have a nervous breakdown?"

"To relax. Go in there," he said, lifting his chin to indicate his bathroom. "Fill the whirlpool tub. Turn on the jets and sit there for thirty minutes."

"But—"

"If Sammi and I need you, we'll get you. Otherwise, you're not to worry. That's an order."

Kelly felt that she should protest a little longer before she gave in, but the suggestion was just too heavenly.

"I'll see you in thirty minutes."

When the time was up, Kelly felt rested and relaxed. She put on shorty pajamas and a thigh-length, lightweight cotton robe. Before leaving her sanctuary, she put her ear to the door and listened, surprised at the quiet. It might be safe, she thought turning off the light as she left the steamy room.

"Mike?" she said softly, walking into the bedroom. The sight that greeted her was just too sweet for words.

Mike was on the bed, half-reclining with pillow shams behind his back, dozing. With one hand on Sammi's back and the other on her rear end, he held her securely on his chest, over his heart. She was also sleeping—like a baby, just the way Kelly's fantasy always played out.

Carefully she moved his arms away and lifted the infant, tucking her into the bassinet, with a light receiving blanket over her. Kelly decided against taking her up to her crib. For one thing, she was afraid the movement might wake her. For another, she was still a bit sore from the birth and didn't feel up to climbing the stairs.

But now she was really in a pickle. She didn't want to be too far from the baby in case she needed something. And she didn't have the heart to wake Mike and ask him to give up his bed. Her only alternative was to sleep there, too.

It was a big bed. There was more than enough room for two people. They could rattle around in it forever and not touch each other. She hoped that was true, because if she touched him, she would be a goner.

Kelly turned out the lights, then removed her robe and slipped between the soft cool sheets. Beside her, she could feel the warmth from Mike's body and hear his even breathing. It took every ounce of her willpower to scoot away from him instead of cuddling up to the strength and security Mike offered.

A knot of fear tightened in her chest. She was terribly attracted to Mike, and she no longer had her pregnancy to keep him at arm's length. The more she was attracted to him, the closer she came to forfeiting his friendship forever. The thought made her feel cold and empty inside. She wanted to take her baby and leave. That's the only thing that would save what she had with Mike.

She couldn't do it.

Sammi had to come first. She had married Mike to be part of a couple and thwart Doug's attempt to take custody. She couldn't do anything to jeopardize that strategy.

This was a fine state of affairs. No, bad choice of word. *Situation* or *mess* would be better. She had landed herself right between the devil and the deep blue sea. If she stayed with Mike, she could lose him. If she left him, she might forfeit her baby.

She curled up into a tight ball. There was only one solution. She had to stay with him until Sammi's custody was no longer in question. He sighed in his sleep and moved restlessly beside her. The pleasant fragrance of his soap and the warmth of his body radiated to her.

Kelly slid to the very edge of the mattress. She would keep her distance from Mike. Ha, she thought. A fine plan when he was sleeping less than a foot away. Emotional distance, she reminded herself.

Her hormones just needed a severe lecturing. She was a teacher; she was a woman. She could keep everything under control. If she was careful, she could have it all.

Mike fought the urge to open his eyes. If the warm, soft, obviously female body snuggling against him was part of an erotic dream, he didn't want to wake up. On the other hand, if he was wrong, and he wasn't sleeping, he wanted to savor the moment.

Her sigh convinced him he wasn't dreaming. As well as the heat, the sensuous sound went spiraling through him. He didn't have to open his eyes to know who the womanly body belonged to. He would know Kelly's scent in a roomful of people, and it surrounded him now. It wasn't just her fragrance that touched him. She had one slender leg carelessly tossed over his, and her hand lightly rested on his abdomen. Half-turned toward him, he could feel the smooth fullness of her breast, covered by some thin, almost nonexistent material, pressed against the muscle in his upper arm.

He didn't question what miracle had landed her in his bed, he just knew he wasn't alone. And he liked it.

Moonlight slicing past the drapes illuminated her beside him. Her dark hair spilled like silk across the pillow, and her thick lashes fanned out above her cheeks. Her full mouth, relaxed in sleep, drew his attention in a big way. The taste of her lips lingered in his memory, tempting him until he couldn't resist. He needed to kiss her as much as he needed to take his next breath. Maybe more.

"Kelly?"

"Hmmm?" she answered sleepily.

"I'm going to kiss you. If you have any objections, speak now."

"Uh-uh," she said shaking her head in a negative motion, though her eyes remained closed.

He rolled slightly, then lowered his mouth to hers. The contact was slow and lazy. Then he gathered her against him, savoring the way her breasts burned into his chest. With his tongue he traced her lips, and she opened to him. He slipped inside and stroked the sweetness there. Kelly's moan of desire fueled the embers of the fire inside him that he'd kept carefully banked all these weeks.

He slid his hand into her hair, cupping the back of her head to make the contact of their mouths more firm. Her arms went around him and caressed his back until he thought he'd go crazy from need. He cautioned himself to patience and pulled the shreds of his self-control together. She had just had a baby. But he suspected Kelly needed the closeness, the touching, as much as he did. It didn't have to be more, not until she was ready.

Mike slid his hand from her silky hair, down her slender throat, to her chest. Her breast filled his palm and she sighed into his mouth, a sound of pure female satisfaction. He went hot all over and his breathing went from zero to sixty in a heartbeat. He knew he had to stop, making love was out of the question. But it felt so good to hold her, feel her against him. If her response was anything to go by, she didn't plan to jump out of bed anytime soon.

He pressed his mouth to the hollow beneath her ear and felt her shiver.

"Kelly," he whispered. "You feel so soft, so good."

She went still and stiff in his arms. It was as if his voice had disturbed the sensuous spell surrounding them.

"Mike?" In the semi-darkness her eyes looked huge, and frightened. "What are you doing?"

"Kissing you. I told you I was going to."

She slid away from him and sat up. "I didn't hear you say that."

"I thought you were awake."

"Did I answer you?" Furrows appeared between her eyebrows as if she couldn't remember what had happened.

"Yeah. Sort of."

Mike didn't want her to think he would take advantage of her, although in reality that's just what he'd done. He wouldn't have, if she hadn't been there beside him.

"I woke up and you were next to me," he said, attempting to explain his behavior.

She nodded as if events had just cleared in her mind. "I put the baby down in here because I was afraid she would wake up if I tried to get her in her crib. I was afraid I wouldn't hear her if I went upstairs. I—" She threw the sheet off and slipped out of bed. Grabbing her robe, she peeked into the bassinet, touched the baby gently, lovingly, then left the room.

Mike got up and looked at the baby. She was still asleep although moving restlessly. He pulled a white T-shirt over his head and went to find Kelly.

She stood in the kitchen, her back to him, her forearms resting on the tile counter.

"What's wrong, Kel?" As if he didn't know. She probably thought he was the slime of the earth. She would be right.

"I'm sorry, Mike."

That surprised him. "Why?"

"For bothering you. I just couldn't face going upstairs. If I didn't hear the baby she would disturb you. It's such a big bed. I thought you wouldn't even know I was there."

Fat chance, he thought. Even if she hadn't cozied up to him, he knew sooner or later he'd have sensed her sweet little body next to his. That kiss had jet-propelled them into something different. He wouldn't call it love, he didn't believe in it. But that kiss was hot enough to fry bacon. He knew she had felt it, too.

"I'm sorry—"

"There's no reason to apologize. I'm not mad," he said. Her shoulders lifted as she took a deep, shuddering breath. "What's wrong, Kelly? This is more than you waking up in my bed. It's about the kiss—"

She whirled around. "Mike, you mustn't ever do that again."

"You kissed me back. Don't tell me you didn't like it."

"I wasn't going to. Just the opposite. I liked it a lot."

"Me, too." He smiled. When he reached a hand out to touch her cheek, she dodged away. A frown pulled his eyebrows together. "I don't understand the problem."

"I've sworn off men. Remember?"

"Yeah. But you also said it wasn't permanent."

"That's true. But it's too soon, Mike. I just had a baby—"

"Wait just a damn minute. What kind of insensitive jerk do you take me for? You didn't think I was going to press you to—"

"No, of course not. I was talking emotionally, not physically."

"I should hope so. But I still don't get what the problem is."

"I'm tired, Mike. My defenses are down. It would be easy to make a mistake with you. I won't risk it."

"What mistake?"

"When Sammi's custody is settled and my life is back on track, I want a relationship with a man."

"What am I? A tackle dummy?"

He was rewarded with a small smile. "I want to find romantic love with someone."

"That's a fantasy, Kel."

"Wouldn't be my first," she said, her lip lifting in a self-derisive expression.

"Don't tell me you're not attracted to me. I just kissed you and you're not that good an actress. If you didn't like it as much as I did— Well, I know for a fact that you know the moves to get yourself out of that kind of situation."

"I wasn't going to deny that I felt...something. But you're not just another pretty face. Not to me. I don't want to make another foolish mistake, especially with you. You're my best friend. What would I do without you?" She tried to make her voice light, but couldn't quite carry it off.

"You're not ever going to lose me, Kel."

"I'm not willing to risk it by complicating things between us. I want your promise that this will never happen again."

Mike wasn't sure he wanted to do what she asked. The kiss they'd shared had sparked something in him that he'd never experienced before. Why shouldn't they explore these feelings and see where it went?

His gaze dropped to Kelly's mouth, still swollen from his kiss, and he knew he couldn't promise her what she asked.

"Define *this*," he said, stalling.

"This," she said, spreading her arms wide. "You know. In your bed."

"Okay. You have my word."

She released a big breath and smiled. "Thanks, Mike."

"Don't mention it."

A whimpering cry came from the bedroom. "Sounds like Sammi is awake. I better change her diaper before I feed her."

Mike watched her back as she left the room. He supposed he couldn't blame her for being cautious, after the mess with Hammond. But she admitted she wanted romantic love someday. He didn't think that love existed, yet he could no longer ignore the power of his feelings for Kelly. He wouldn't label it. He wouldn't spoil things by doing that. He also wouldn't throw away this opportunity with her while they were together.

When she had said she wanted to find romantic love with someone, Mike had been surprised at the jealousy that roared through him. Maybe he wasn't the most romantic guy in the world, but he was competitive. He could damn well learn.

Thoughts tumbled through his mind. Sammi's birth had convinced him of two things—he wanted to be around to protect her and watch her grow up and he needed Kelly in his life.

Kelly didn't want to complicate their relationship. She was kidding herself if she thought it wasn't already confusing. They could try to go back to what they had before tonight's kiss. There was a part of Mike that really wanted to do just that, to run like hell in the other direction. He was a trained competitor and he liked winning. He had made big mistakes in the relationship department, and he didn't like failing. If he didn't play again, he couldn't lose. But he couldn't win, either. And he hadn't counted on one thing.

How wonderful it was to kiss Kelly.

He couldn't possibly let her go now. He had a little

time left; there must be something he could do. The only thing worse than losing would be to wonder what might have been. He had to make every second count.

If she wanted romance, he would give her romance.

Chapter Eight

"You're up to something, Mike Cameron."

"What makes you think that?" he asked, shoving the brown bag behind his back.

"That look of exaggerated innocence on your face for one thing," she said, pointing straight at his nose. "My second clue is that you don't normally sneak purchases in small brown bags into the house. And you're not very good at it. Don't quit your day job to work for the CIA."

"I hadn't planned to."

"What is that?" She leaned to the side, trying to see the package and figure out what he'd brought. It could be Chinese food from China Palace down the street, but there was no mouth-watering smell. Besides, why hide egg rolls?

He put the bag in front of him and went into the kitchen, but Kelly dogged his steps every inch of the way, all the while stretching as high as she could to look over his broad shoulder to get a glimpse of the package. Why did he have to be so darn big? It was like trying to peek around a mountain.

One stride ahead of her in the kitchen, he put the bag in the refrigerator and slammed the door shut. He positioned himself in front of it and crossed his arms over his wide chest like an Egyptian soldier guarding the pharaoh.

"What are you up to, Mike?" she asked again, narrowing her eyes at him.

"Nothing."

"Okay, let's forget the mysterious package for now. Why did Susan call and tell me she and Brad would be here at six-thirty this evening?"

"To baby-sit."

"Why? I'll be here."

"No, you won't."

"Why not?"

"Because you're going out."

"I can't leave Sammi. She's only three weeks old. She's too little."

"Closer to four weeks, and I anticipated this evasive move of yours. I already checked with the pediatrician and he said there's no reason why you can't leave her with someone you trust. You trust Susan. Right?"

"Well, yes, but her children are out of high school now. She hasn't taken care of an infant in a long time."

He grinned. "I anticipated that, too. She said it's like riding a bike. You never forget."

"It's a terrible imposition."

"She said she'd love to do it." He raised one eyebrow and shot her a challenging look. "That's three. You get seven more excuses."

He had come up with ten reasons why they should get married, and he'd won. She had a feeling he'd be victorious this time, too, but she couldn't help smiling at him. This was exhilarating. And more stimulating than talking to an infant who couldn't talk back, cute though Sammi might be. Kelly decided to play his game.

She thought for a minute. "What if Sammi has a crisis and I can't get to her?"

"I've got the cellular phone, and where we're going, we can be home in fifteen minutes."

"So we're not going out of the valley?"

"Nope. And I'm not going to tell you where, either, so get that look off your face," he said.

"Look who's talking about looks, Mr. Innocent Expression." She thought again. "Sammi's fussy time is six to eleven. What if Susan doesn't know what to do?"

"That's excuse number five and six, and the last one is reaching a little," he said, rocking his hand back and forth like a plane dipping its wings. "Give her a list of all the tricks you use to quiet Little Bit. Susan's a competent adult. She'll be fine."

"What about all the cracks she made about doing away with kids while they're still smaller than she is?"

"She was joking. You know how frustrating teenagers can be. Besides, we won't be gone that long, and if she's ready to tear her hair out, she can call us."

"What if the phone doesn't work?"

"We'll test it. But if necessary, we can use pay phones every fifteen minutes until she really is ready to tear her hair out and yours, too." He stared intently at her. "You've got three excuses left, and if none of them are any better than those, you're going out tonight even if I have to throw you over my shoulder and kidnap you."

"I'm out of shape, and I have nothing to wear."

His gaze dropped to her mouth, then the spaghetti strap T-shirt over her chest, a little lower to her almost flat abdomen and finally her legs below her short shorts. The whole process took a matter of a few seconds, but Kelly felt as if time had stopped. Heat flowed through her, making her cheeks burn. She was almost glad that he was still looking at her ankles. Her pulse raced, and she put a hand to her throat, a protective gesture to keep Mike from seeing that little vein in her neck throb. If he saw, he would know that one of his looks made her heart race as if she'd done a five-K run.

"You're in terrific shape. I've seen you take Sammi out in the jogging stroller. And even if you weren't back to fighting weight, I'm sure you've got a loose dress you could wear."

"So I need to wear a dress?"

"No. I just thought that might be cool and comfortable. I still plan to surprise you. No information from me," he said. "You've got one more excuse, Kelly. Make it good."

It was the best reason of all. "This is too much like a date, Mike."

"A date? Perish the thought," he answered.

"It feels like it to me, and as far as I'm concerned, *date* is a four-letter word."

"Well, it's not a date."

She shot him a skeptical look. "Oh, yeah? It has all the earmarks of one."

He snorted. "First of all married people don't go on dates. Second, we're friends—a man and a woman going out to eat together because one of them needs R & R before she turns into a hermit crab."

"Me?" she said, touching her chest.

"You," he answered, easing away from the refrigerator to touch her collarbone, just above her hand. "I'm getting the feeling that you don't want to go out with me. Or are you afraid to?"

All of the above, she thought. His finger lightly stroked the base of her throat, sending tingles skidding through her.

Their bodies were inches apart, and Kelly could feel the warmth of his heating her from head to toe. She flashed back on that kiss they'd shared in his bed. Countless times over the last weeks she'd wanted to tell him to forget the promise she'd wrung from him. She'd wanted him to kiss her like that again. But every time she was tempted, she'd reminded herself it was dangerous.

She had stayed out of his way as much as possible. For a good reason. When they were together, she wanted to blurt out, "Kiss me you fool," like some sappy character from an old movie. She'd had to bite her tongue. Hard. But she dared anyone to say a woman couldn't keep her mouth shut!

"Me? Afraid of you? Perish the thought," she said, echoing his own words. Unlike his calm voice, hers sounded too high, too shaky and too unconvincing.

"That means I don't have to play the Neanderthal to take you out to dinner?"

"So we're going to dinner?"

"I'll take that as a yes." He started to walk out of the kitchen. "It was never a secret that we were going to dinner. The surprise is where we're going and what's in that refrigerator." He gave her a stern look, the one designed to keep his players in training before a big game. "Don't peek in there. And don't think I won't know if you do. You're not a good liar, and you couldn't act your way out of a paper bag.''

''So you keep telling me,'' she said wryly, knowing he was referring to their kiss.

She hadn't been able to conceal her feelings then. She hoped her Thespian skills had improved some. Because as much as she knew she should refuse to go out to dinner with him, she couldn't.

The idea of time to herself was too tempting. She tried to tell herself it would be just as appealing if she were going to a movie with Susan and the girls. But Mike was right. She was a lousy liar. The thought of being alone with him for an evening sent tingles of eager anticipation coursing through her. They were a man and woman going out for a meal. After all, she had to eat.

But it was *not* a date.

''See? The phone works. Even here in the restaurant in the canyon,'' Mike said, placing the cellular on the white tablecloth beside him.

The candle in the crystal holder between them flickered, sending out shards of rainbow-tinged light that illuminated just the two of them. Other couples were just dim shapes around them, creating the impression they were the only two people in the place.

Kelly looked beautiful in her black-and-white sundress. The thin straps left her arms bare, and the low neckline gave him just a hint of her tempting curves. Her shiny brown hair just barely touched her creamy shoulders, and her green eyes sparkled with enjoyment.

Le Chêne's wood walls and beam ceilings perfectly suited the romantic mood Mike was creating tonight. He wanted to make points with her, and he knew this restaurant was her favorite. He figured the score on his side of the board was climbing steadily. Now if only he could put her mind to rest about Sammi.

"Thanks for letting me check on her, Mike. And for the flowers, too," she said, lightly touching the white rose corsage on her wrist.

"You're welcome." The pensive expression on her face worried him. He wondered if his gift had upset her. "Is something bothering you?" he asked. "If you're still concerned about Sammi—"

"No. At least it's not an immediate worry. Susan sounded fine just now." She grinned suddenly. "She's teaching Sammi to talk."

"Good luck," he said.

"She thinks Sammi's really bright."

"I'm sure she is. After all, you're her mother. But as a teacher you know as well as I do that readiness is an issue."

"I know. But if it makes Susan happy, the stimulation has to be good for the baby." Her smile faded as she looked at him.

"What is it, Kel?"

She rested her hand on the table, beside her silverware. "I talked to the lawyer today about the custody hearing."

"And?"

"He says he's taking care of everything and not to worry."

"Then what's wrong?"

She shrugged. "I guess I wanted more facts, something concrete to convince me that everything will be fine."

Mike felt a stab of guilt. He knew what was going on. A plan was in the works, but there was nothing hard-and-fast yet that would put her mind at ease. Until Doug agreed to drop his custody suit, Mike would do whatever was necessary, including keeping Kelly in the dark. She wasn't pregnant anymore, but that didn't lessen his need to protect her. If anything, he felt it more keenly.

Mike covered her hand with his own. "If Tim says he has everything under control, then I'm sure he does. The wheels of justice are square. There's a lot of down-time when a legal eagle has his beak stuck in a book. Tim is one of the best in the business."

"I know you've told me that but—"

He met her gaze and willed her to believe him. "I'd trust him with my life. More important, I trust him with Sammi. Don't you trust me?"

"Of course, but—"

"No *buts*. Relax. You're not going to lose custody of her."

"I hope you're right. And I'm trying not to worry. But this waiting is driving me nuts. I want to relax and enjoy my baby without worrying about whether or not she'll be with me."

"You can do that." He squeezed her fingers.

Kelly was relieved when the waiter brought their salads and Mike was forced to release his hold on her. In spite of his assurances to the contrary, this seemed a lot like a date to her.

She hadn't seen him this dressed up since their wedding. In his yellow sports shirt and beige slacks, he looked awfully handsome. His dark hair was neatly combed back, except for the one lock that wouldn't stay tamed and insisted on curling over his forehead. It had been dangerous to accept his invitation tonight, no matter what she called it. *Date* was definitely a four-letter word. So was *hell*.

Although he kept denying it, she was sure he was up to something. He couldn't act any better than she could.

She decided to test him.

"Did you know Le Chêne is my favorite restaurant?"

He looked at her over the rim of his water goblet and his dark eyebrows went up in an expression of such exaggerated innocence that she knew he knew. All he said was, "Really?"

She nodded. "It was very sweet of you to bring me here. And the flowers. Why, if I didn't know better and I wasn't a nursing mother, I'd swear phase two of tonight's plan would be to ply me with alcohol and have your way with me."

She narrowed her gaze on him, studying his response in order to judge his truthfulness.

When he finished chewing and set down his fork, his expression was the essence of honesty. Even before he spoke, Kelly was beginning to feel like the slime of the earth.

"I've always been straightforward with you, Kelly."

"I know. I'm sorry."

"Besides, you gave me your permission to date other women if the need arose."

"You're right. I'd forgotten."

She would bet her last nickel he hadn't been with another woman, but jealousy rose up inside her at the idea. She'd never felt that way before, and it scared her.

"I'd never ply you with alcohol."

"I know that. I apologize, Mike."

A wounded look drew his mouth down. "You keep accusing me of having ulterior motives. I'm hurt, Kelly."

"I'm sorry. How many times do I have to say it? What else can I do?"

"I'm not sure. Give me time. I'll think of something. Later," he said.

There was a gleam in his eyes that Kelly wasn't sure she liked. In the past, pizza and burgers had been the extent of their commingling at mealtime. Mike was a nice guy, but an expensive French restaurant was pushing things, even for him.

She wasn't worried that he would hurt her. He wouldn't, at least not deliberately. But she couldn't shake the feeling that he had something up his sleeve besides a powerful bicep.

"So what do you think?" Mike asked, watching her as she stared at the valley below them.

"It's breathtaking," she said.

Kelly knew better than to go up to Sunset Point with Mike Cameron, but the magic of the night had cast a spell that seemed to rob her of the ability to say no. The baby was fine; Susan was fine. She couldn't think of a reason to deny herself a little more free time. The fact was she hadn't wanted to say no. As soon as he'd mentioned the idea, she couldn't wait to get there.

And here they were, standing in front of his Bronco, looking down at the Santa Clarita Valley all lit up like a Christmas tree. A pleasant breeze lifted the hair from her neck and cooled her flushed cheeks.

Mike's shoulder brushed hers as he pointed. "There's the high school, and the house is over in that direction."

"The whole world looks different from up here." It was spectacular, she thought, studying Mike's handsome profile in the moonlight. She sighed. Life would be so much easier if only he looked like Quasimodo. But Esmeralda had seen past Mr. Q.'s grotesque exterior to the generous person underneath. Mike had a heart as grand as the view that stretched before them and looks to match. A lethal combination as far as Kelly was concerned.

"How did you know about this place?" she asked, a slightly breathless quality in her voice.

"From the guys. It's the local make-out spot."

"Aha. I knew you were up to something."

"I never guessed that you were so suspicious. The only thing I'm up to is giving you a short rest from motherhood. You know what they say about all work and no play."

Mike looked down at her, and something smoldered in his eyes. It set off sparks deep inside Kelly, and suddenly she wanted very much to play. A warning buzzed through her like a smoke detector in a hazy room. She tuned it out. She would worry about everything later. Right this minute she just wanted to *feel*.

He reached over and threaded his fingers into her loose hair, cupping the back of her head. Kelly knew he was going to kiss her, and if it meant saving her life, she knew she didn't have the will to stop him.

When his mouth tentatively touched hers, she sighed with contentment. She felt as if she had been drifting in an open sea and the Coast Guard had just towed her back to port, and home.

Gently he moved his lips over hers, letting her feel the soft, warm sweetness. Flutters started in her stomach, like a flurry of hummingbirds. Suddenly he was in front of her, his arm around her waist pulling her snugly against his muscular length. Her breath caught as she slipped her arms around his neck and felt her breasts pressed to the hard wall of his chest.

Yearning, as powerful and elemental as the need to breathe, welled up inside her, squeezing out everything but Mike. His heat, the heady fragrance of him, his heart beating the same wild rhythm as her own.

As if they were one.

When his tongue gently nudged the seam of her lips, she opened to him eagerly. He slipped inside and caressed her, setting off a tingling that started in her chest and worked its way down to her toes, making her feel as if her legs wouldn't hold her weight. But Mike would never let her fall.

He pressed his mouth to her cheek and trailed kisses along her jaw and touched a spot just beneath her ear that drew a moan from her. She heard his labored breathing and felt the rapid rise and fall of his chest.

She pulled away from him, just far enough to look into his eyes. "You promised not to kiss me like that again," she said. She whispered so softly, so seductively, that the disapproval she'd tried to put in her words just wasn't there.

"I promised not to kiss you in the bed."

"You're splitting hairs."

"I'm sorry. But it's your fault," he said.

"Mine?"

He leaned back against the car and tugged her in front of him, settling her between his legs, his hands loosely holding her waist. "You're so beautiful."

"I don't think you've ever told me that before."

"Sure I have."

"Well, maybe when I was dressed up for a special

occasion you might have said something, but not just out of the blue. Why now?'' she asked.

"I don't know. I thought it, so I said it.''

"But I don't look any different than I ever have. What's going on, Mike?''

He shrugged. "Must be motherhood. It agrees with you.''

"I think you're imagining things. Besides, the discussion is pointless. We have to stop this right now.''

"Define *this*,'' he said.

"This,'' she answered, taking his hands from her waist. "Kissing.''

"We were necking like a couple of teenagers. What do you suppose the kids would say if they saw us?''

"There won't be anything to see, because we're going to stop. Right now. We can't do this.''

"Why?'' he asked, tracing the thin strap of her dress.

She pulled her shoulder back, away from his fingers. "Because when you do things like that I can't think straight—''

"You think too much.'' She started to say something and he gently touched his index finger to her lips, silencing her. "You were about to tell me that I don't think enough. Maybe that's true. But I know for a fact that you talk too much.''

Before she could retort, he lowered his mouth to hers, this time quieting her with a kiss. The words on the tip of her tongue were forgotten, like always when he touched her. Her body had a mind and language of its own. As she nestled in the circle of his arms, she knew his body was carrying on the same conversation when she felt his arousal.

Her breath caught. Like sudden lightning in the sky, the thought struck her. Mike Cameron wanted to make love. With her. Then the thunder rattled her. She wanted him, too.

"Kelly?" he said, his voice breathless and husky.

"What?" she answered.

"Remember that promise I made about kissing you like this—"

"What about it?"

"You forced it out of me," he said, nibbling her ear. She shivered. "I know."

"I think I have to take it back."

"According to the rules of friendship—"

"No." He stopped kissing her neck, and his hands tightened at her waist. Straightening, he stared down at her, a dark intensity making his features almost harsh in the moonlight. "Stop hiding from life behind the word *friendship*."

"That's ridiculous."

"Is it? There's something going on between us, and you're refusing to acknowledge it."

"No, I'm not. I'll even give it a name. It's called *lust*," she said, trying to be flippant.

"It's more than that. I want you, Kelly. I think you know that. But I care about you, and it's different—"

"Don't say it."

"Why not? Because you want me, too?"

"I do. But—"

"I know it's too soon after the baby. And when we make love it won't be in the back seat of a car like a couple of teenagers. It will be in our bed—"

"We can't, Mike." She stepped away from him and went to the passenger side of the Bronco. She opened the door and climbed inside.

Mike got in beside her. "Why?"

"We have an agreement. When the marriage ends,

we go our separate ways. If we give in to our hormones, that will just muddle up everything.''

He let out a long breath as he ran his fingers through his hair. "Not everything in life is neat and tidy, Kelly.''

"There's one thing that is.''

"What's that?'' he asked.

"Our friendship.''

Chapter Nine

The day after Mike crashed and burned in the romance department, he picked up his video camera and started filming everything in sight. He told himself it was just to fill the time until football started up again, and to practice his photography skills for taping the games. But the reality was that someone else filmed the games, and he wasn't looking forward to the season as much as usual. On top of that, the end of summer was approaching and he couldn't stop it.

When school started again, Kelly and Sammi would be gone.

It was like waiting for the other shoe to drop. You knew it would be bad, you just didn't know how bad until it smacked you.

He had spoken to the lawyer about the custody hearing, which Kelly knew nothing about. With luck she would never have to know it had even been scheduled until the whole thing was dropped. Tim was setting the wheels of a plan in motion that would force Hammond to put up or shut up. Mike was betting on the latter. That was the good news.

The bad was that when that happened, Kelly would hold him to their agreement, which meant she would leave with the baby and file for divorce.

The D-word sounded so ugly when it involved Kelly. Divorce was no more than Carol had deserved. When his pro career had ended, he had told her he wanted to work with kids, to teach and coach. She had suggested sportscasting or something in the media. She'd said he had the looks for it and should use what he had.

But Mike knew if it hadn't been for the Walker family, he would have wound up a loser. They had taken a mixed-up kid into their home and set him on a positive path, using sports. He wanted to give back, to help kids. When he told Carol, she laughed. She assumed he was kidding. He wasn't.

His glory days were gone and so was she. He didn't like losing at anything, and he had gone into the relationship with every intention of making it last. In the end he'd had to admit he hadn't been hurt. In fact, he hadn't missed her or given her absence more than a passing thought.

With Kelly everything was different. He laughed more, he felt more, he talked more. He had jokingly told her that he was lonely. After knowing what a family was like, he had found out that it was no joke. The idea of life without Kelly and Sammi seemed hollow and empty.

He heard Kelly running water upstairs and knew it was bath time. He knew the drill. Afterward, Sammi would take her morning nap. He grabbed the video from the bar in the kitchen and took the stairs two at a time.

On the tile countertop, Kelly had set up a small, inflatable rubber tub and filled it with water. She was just lowering the baby into it when he started filming.

Kelly met his gaze in the mirror. "Look who's here, Sammi. It's your Uncle Mike."

He gritted his teeth. It really fried him when she called him that. In the days since their nondate, she'd been doing it more frequently. That whole evening had really backfired. Kelly was looking for romantic love, and that fiasco had no doubt convinced her that he wasn't the man who could give it to her. Instead of the thrill of victory, he kept having his nose rubbed in the agony of defeat.

The towel bar dug into his back as he shifted to the side a bit to get a better angle of the baby. "Kel, can you lower your shoulder a little and lift her so *Uncle* Mike can get a better shot of her face?"

At his tone she raised one eyebrow, but did as he'd asked. The corners of her full mouth lifted, and she grinned broadly at the baby. "Smile into the camera, Sammi."

"Isn't she a little young for that?"

"She's just starting to."

"It's gas." He couldn't resist baiting her.

He knew it worked when her gaze met his in the mirror. But when she spoke, her voice was teasing. "That's most unladylike. This little girl gets bubbles."

"That turn into smiles."

"No. I can actually get her to smile. It's exhausting, but if circumstances are just right, I can get one out of her."

Mike kept the camera going. With a wide smile plastered on her face, and talking in a singsong voice, Kelly coaxed a fleeting, toothless grin from the baby.

"Did you get that?" Kelly asked excitedly.

"You bet I did," he answered.

"Oh, Mike. Her first real smile. I can't wait to see it again."

"When you finish her bath and put her down, I'll set this up on the TV."

"This water's cooling off. I'll have her out of here in a jiffy. Right, Little Bit?" she said, her expression soft and loving as she stared at the baby. "I didn't know it was possible to feel this way," she said, her voice trembling with emotion.

"What way?" he asked.

"So much love. When she's quiet and content, it makes me ache inside. And when she's fussy I just want to make everything better. I want to make her world a perfect place. If anyone ever hurt her—"

Mike pressed the camera's On button and captured the look on Kelly's face. He had never seen anything like it. Simple and soft, yet powerful and profound. It was proof that love really existed. He couldn't remember seeing anyone look at him like that. The closest he'd come to knowing affection was when he'd lived with the Walkers. That family knew how to care.

Because of them Kelly believed in love and was looking for it. Everywhere but with him.

She expertly cradled the baby's head in the crook of her elbow, leaving both hands free to hold a cloth and put soap on it. While Mike filmed, she washed the infant, who stared contentedly, blissfully unaware of the tension around her.

"What are you going to do with all the film you've been taking?" Kelly asked him.

"I hadn't thought about it."

"I'd like to have it, or a copy if you want the original."

"I'll make you a copy."

"On my first date, my mother embarrassed me with naked baby pictures. I wouldn't do that to Sammi, but just think of the motivational possibilities. Clean your room, or your boyfriend sees you on TV, in the flesh." She glanced over her shoulder and grinned.

The beauty of her smile caught him unexpectedly, like a blindside tackle. Instinctively he kept filming, partly because he didn't want her to see the look on his face. If it was anything like the feeling in his gut, she would know he didn't want her to take her copy of the film and go.

Without telling him straight-out to butt out, Kelly was letting him know that she planned to raise Samantha by herself. He had captured the baby's first smile on tape. But when that little girl took her first steps, said her first words, went to school on the first day, or had her first date he wouldn't be there.

God, he hated the thought of that.

He *wanted* to be there. He wanted to protect her, guide her, watch out for her. He realized that blood ties didn't matter a tinker's damn. He wanted to be a father to Sammi, in every way that counted. But Kelly seemed to think that was an imposition, and she had to do it on her own. And she was stubborn and proud enough to do just that.

Unless he could somehow convince her to extend, or even better, annul their agreement and stay.

That would give them time to explore their feelings, give them a chance to see if this relationship thing could work. He refused to call it *love*. One corner of his mouth lifted wryly. Would Kelly call that a four-letter word? Or would she think of it that way only if it referred to him? He didn't like labels. He didn't want to put the whammy on what he felt for Kelly by naming it.

He lowered the camera. She called it *friendship,* neat and tidy. He planned to find out if it was more than that.

After bathing and feeding Sammi, Kelly put her down for a nap. She smiled as the baby grinned in her sleep. That probably was gas. It reminded her of Mike's comments as he'd videotaped. It warmed her heart that he had taken the time to record her hard-won smile. Since Sammi's birth, he had been Kelly's idea of what a perfect father would be. He hadn't let her down once.

Why that would make her uneasy around him, she couldn't say, but she had been since the night they'd gone to Le Chêne. The words ''nervous as a long-tailed cat in a room full of rocking chairs'' came to mind. It was a cliché, and as a teacher she encouraged her students to be fresh and creative. But just the same, the saying was appropriate.

Mike was trying to change the rules of their friendship, of their agreement. He hadn't told her straight-out, but she sensed a tension between them that she'd never felt before. The worst part was that she was tempted to let him change things, go along with him and see where it would lead. If she were a fly-by-the-seat-of-her-sweatpants type of person, she might. But she wasn't. She was the outline and execute type. Stick to the plan.

Mike had been married before. He'd fallen out of

love with his wife and divorced her. Now he never even mentioned her name. Kelly knew it would break her heart if they took that step into an intimate relationship, then she had to watch helplessly as it fell apart. She didn't think she could stand it if he put her out of his life that way. Maybe he was right when he'd said she was hiding behind the word *friendship*. But she wasn't willing to take it over the line. Losing Mike wasn't part of her plan.

At the sound of the doorbell, Kelly raced to the front door. Mike was in the backyard trimming the oleander behind the pool. It usually took Sammi a while to fall soundly asleep, and Kelly was afraid the noise would startle her awake. Then she would never settle. It would throw her schedule off.

She had a hard enough time keeping her on a time-table, because Mike was forever waking her up to play. It was hard to get mad at him for giving the baby so much attention, though. Especially when she didn't have a father.

Kelly opened the front door, and her stomach lurched when she saw Doug Hammond standing there.

"Hi, Kel."

"I told you never to call me that," she snapped.

"Old habits die hard," he said, shrugging. Dressed in tennis shorts and a blue golf shirt, he looked the part of up-and-coming attorney on his day off, ready to tee off. The sight of him really teed her off.

She couldn't believe that she had once been susceptible to his lean, blond good looks. Now that she knew him for the underhanded manipulator he was, she couldn't stand to look at him. Anyone who would use a baby to get a promotion was pretty low.

"What do you want?" she asked.

"Would you believe I want to talk to you about my little girl?"

"No," she said coldly.

She hoped to God she was right. In her heart she believed the custody suit would fall apart because he didn't truly care about the baby. Through legal channels he had been notified about Sammi's birth. She was four weeks old, and he hadn't called or come to see her until now.

But what if she was wrong about his indifference toward the baby? She and Sammi would never be free of him.

"Well, I do want to talk about her. I'm her father, after all."

"A fact I'm trying hard to ignore."

He braced a hand on the doorjamb. "Aren't you going to invite me in, Mrs. Cameron?"

"No." She winced at the use of her married name. Did he know the marriage was an act? He couldn't. Only she and Mike knew.

"Are you going to tell me her name?"

"I figured you already knew."

He shook his head. "I was only notified of her birth, no other details."

"And you waited until now to ask?"

"I've been busy. Are you going to tell me the child's name?"

"The child? That has all the warmth of a Sno-Kone, Doug." Exactly the reason she would do whatever she had to, so that he wouldn't get his hands on Sammi.

"What did you name her?"

"Samantha Michele. As if you care."

"Of course I care," he said. The words were just this side of sarcastic and definitely lacking sincerity. "I thought I should know my daughter's name for the court hearing next week.''

Kelly gasped. Then she couldn't make a sound. She felt as if a boulder the size of a house was crushing her chest. She hadn't heard anything about a court date. Why hadn't her lawyer informed her?

"From the expression on your face, I'd guess you didn't know about it. What kind of lawyer did you retain, Kelly?"

"He's a friend of Mike's."

"Ah," he said. "A gridiron gorilla with more brawn than brains."

"You're wrong, Doug. Tim Sargent is an expert in family law."

"Maybe. But it hardly does him or you any good if he fails to instruct his client on important court appearances."

Doug was right. Kelly had no defense for that, so she decided to change the subject.

"You're not here to point out my attorney's faults, and you're not here because you give a damn about the baby. This is all about punishing me because I wouldn't do what you wanted. You won't get away with it, Doug. I'll stop you."

"Is that what your countersuit is all about?" he asked, blue eyes narrowing.

"Countersuit?" Her forehead wrinkled with confusion.

"Yes."

That was the second time in as many minutes that he'd shocked her out of her socks, and she was barefoot. Tim had talked about the possibility of a countersuit, but that was the last he'd told her. She took a deep breath and figured she'd bluff her way through, until she could call that lawyer and find out what in the world was going on.

"My attorney says we can throw everything but the kitchen sink at you," she said.

"You didn't know anything about that, either." He held a hand up. "Don't bother denying it. You're not very good at hiding your feelings."

"So I'm told." She put a hand on her hip. "I'll find out the details. But I'll tell you one thing right now— I'll put up every possible obstacle to block you. Sammi will be out of college before there's a chance in hell that you'll get your hands on her. You'll lose in the long run."

"You're wrong about that."

She lifted her chin a little. "There's a partnership meeting soon, isn't there, Doug?"

"There is," he said, as if it was hardly important to him. "But I'm here to claim my fatherly rights."

"In a pig's eye. You tried to use me to get what you wanted. Now you want to use my daughter. I won't let you get away with it."

Mike walked up beside her and slipped his arm around her waist, pulling her against his warmth. "Get out, Hammond."

Only then did Kelly allow herself to shiver. Mike's strength seemed to flow through her, bracing her. Thank God he was there.

"Aren't you even going to ask why I'm here?" Doug said.

"I know why."

"You do?" Kelly glanced up at him. How could he?

Mike squeezed her waist reassuringly. "If you don't get the hell away from Kelly, you'll regret it."

"I should have known you'd resort to violence."

Doug crossed his arms over his chest, but a vein in his forehead began to throb. Kelly knew he was nervous.

"You'd love for me to throw a punch so you could slap me with an assault-and-battery charge. I wouldn't give you the satisfaction. There are better ways to handle you—legal ways."

Doug's eyes widened as if he'd just figured out the mystery. "Maybe you can explain to Kelly about the court date and the countersuit."

Kelly looked up at Mike again. "What's he talking about?"

"I'll tell you later," Mike said. But he wouldn't meet her gaze, and Kelly knew he was hiding something.

"Why not now, Cameron? Tell her why the attorney you sent her to has kept her in the dark about what's going on."

Mike dropped his arm and glared at the other man. "Don't try to make me out to be the bad guy here." He pointed an accusing finger at Doug. "You slept with your client. You violated the canon of legal ethics *and* breached your fiduciary duty."

Surprised, Doug raised one dark blond eyebrow. "I was right. You've been talking to the lawyer."

Mike shrugged. "I found out the legal terms, but I don't need an attorney to put two-dollar words in my mouth in order to tell you you're scum."

"Slander, Cameron."

"The truth, Hammond."

Kelly knew Mike didn't get those legal terms from a football playbook. As much as she hated to agree with Doug about anything, she was afraid he was right. Mike had been talking to Tim Sargent. And she had been left off the information chain.

Doug's lips straightened to a thin line. "You're behind that countersuit."

"That's right, Counselor." The satisfaction in Mike's voice was unmistakable.

"What's he talking about, Mike?"

A muscle in Doug's cheek contracted angrily. "It's nothing more than a nuisance complaint. It'll never go anywhere in court."

Ignoring her question, Mike stepped toward the other man, who backed up out of the doorway. "Hammond, let's get something straight. You're the guy in the black hat. Bad guys finish last. I'm going to bury you."

"Not with violation of legal ethics and breach of fiduciary duty."

Mike walked over the threshold onto the porch, and for an instant fear flashed in Doug's eyes and his body tensed. When Mike crossed his arms over his chest, the other man let out a small, relieved breath.

Mike moved his shoulders as if he was keeping a tight rein on his temper. "Those are just the grounds for the *civil* complaint. The criminal charges are emotional battery and intentional infliction of emotional distress."

"That's ridiculous—"

"We know we may not get a judgment, but the negative publicity could ruin your reputation or possibly get you disbarred. And make no mistake. There will be a lot of publicity. Local newspapers, which will ruin you in this town. Syndicated newspapers will spread the word in case you decide to look out-of-state for a job. I haven't decided yet whether or not to call a press conference—"

"You wouldn't."

"Yeah, I would. And even though I've been out of

pro ball for a while, I think I could generate enough interest to do what I have to.'' Mike stared hard at the other man, letting the import of his words sink in. ''At the very least you stand a good chance of losing that partnership you're manipulating for.''

''Why, you—''

''What happened to all your two-dollar words, Counselor?''

''You won't get away with this, Cameron.''

''Yeah, I will. The complaint is all drawn up. If you don't drop the custody suit, my lawyer has instructions to file it. When I get through with you, you won't be able to get a partnership in a popcorn stand.''

Doug nervously ran his tongue over his dry lips. ''And if I do drop my claims to the kid?''

''My attorney has another set of briefs drawn up stating that you relinquish any present and future rights to the baby. If you kill the custody suit and sign the papers stating that you will never contact Kelly or her child, the countersuit will be dropped. No one will be the wiser. And you'll probably get your partnership. Much as I'd like to put you out of business permanently, my first priority is Kelly and the baby.''

''How noble of you,'' Doug said sarcastically.

Mike wanted to put his fist square in the guy's patrician nose. Doug needed a shot of character. And that was about the only way he would get any. Nothing would give Mike more pleasure than to mess up this arrogant jerk. He glanced over his shoulder at Kelly. One look at her chalk-white face held him in check.

''So what's it gonna be, Hammond?''

Doug's face was red as he gritted his teeth. He thought for a few seconds before he said, ''You win, Cameron. I'll sign the papers.''

Mike nodded, satisfied. "I can see you're not stupid. Just an underhanded, manipulative, shady weasel."

"Name calling is exactly what I'd expect from a low-class person like you."

"Now just a minute, Doug," Kelly said, brushing past Mike to face the other man.

Mike couldn't hide his grin. He sure didn't need her to come to his defense, but it made this revenge all the sweeter when she did.

She pointed her finger at the other man, and the way her hand shook told Mike she was fighting mad. "Mike Cameron is a lot of things, but low class isn't one of them. That's really the pot calling the kettle black if you ask me."

Doug's lip curled distastefully. "You have to stick up for him. You married this has-been jock, and now you're stuck with him."

Kelly shot Mike a glance that he couldn't read. But when she looked back at Doug her balled fists were trembling with anger. "He's a better man than you could ever hope to be, Doug. He's kind and caring and everything I ever wanted in a father for my child. He's everything you're not, and more."

Doug stared at her, his eyes widening in shock. "I'll be damned. And here I thought you just married him to save your job."

"What are you talking about?" Kelly asked.

"You're actually in love with this two-bit muscle man."

Mike expected her to deny it, but she didn't. Then he realized she couldn't. At least not until he had signed the papers relinquishing custody.

She put her hands on her hips. "We've said everything there is to say, Doug. Please go now."

He nodded. "I suppose there's no point in prolonging this. Goodbye, Kelly." He turned away, then stopped and looked back at her. "For what it's worth, I really do care about you."

"That and a buck will barely buy me a cup of coffee," she said quietly.

Mike stood beside her on the porch as Doug backed his BMW down the driveway.

When the engine sounds had died away, Kelly sighed sadly. "He never even asked to see his daughter."

"He doesn't deserve her." He stared down at her. The breeze pushed her hair off her face. Her eyes were narrowed, and he wondered what she was thinking.

Was she sorry Hammond was out of her life? Did she have any feelings for him? The thought made Mike want to pull her into his arms and make her forget that she'd ever known Doug Hammond. Or was she regretting that Sammi would never know her father? If Mike had anything to say about it, and he would, that little girl would never miss the sorry son of a bitch.

"Sammi's better off without him." He turned to her and touched a finger to the corner of her lip. "Smile. Look on the bright side. You don't have to worry about him anymore, Kel."

"I don't feel like smiling." When she looked up at him, her eyes were blazing. "Don't you 'Kel' me, you traitor. You've got some explaining to do."

"Me?" he said, innocently touching his chest.

"Let's go inside. I need to listen for Sammi."

Mike followed her into the house and closed the door. In the family room she started to pace. She was really ticked off. He knew why and almost wished Hammond was still there insulting him so Kelly would jump to his defense. But now he was on his own and had to figure out how to defend himself to her.

"I had to do it, Kel."

"What?"

"Like Susan said at the wedding, I'm your knight in shining armor, your Sir Walter Raleigh throwing my cloak over the legal swamp—"

"Susan is a romantic—"

"I thought you were, too."

"I can't afford to be. Not anymore. I've sworn off men."

"Not permanently."

"Yes, permanently."

"Since when?"

"Since today, when I found out I can't trust my best friend."

Chapter Ten

Kelly abruptly stopped pacing and stood in front of the fireplace with her arms folded over her chest. When Mike looked into her angry, hurt, green eyes, he wished he could find the words to help him make her understand why he'd done what he had.

He reached out to cup her cheek.

"Don't," she said, ducking her head away.

He sighed. In the past he could always tease or charm her out of it when she was mad. If ever he needed to finesse his moves, now was the time. "Let me take a shot in the dark here. I know you're upset—"

"Upset?" Her eyes grew wide and her voice rose a notch or two. "You can do better than that, Coach. I'm confused, angry, hurt and betrayed. *Upset* doesn't even scratch the surface of what I'm feeling."

"I'm not your enemy." She made him feel like Benedict Arnold. "I can sort of understand the other stuff. But *betrayed?*"

"Let's take that up later. Give me one good reason why you thought you didn't need to tell me that there was a scheduled court date for a hearing on my baby's custody."

"I'll give you ten—"

"And I'll bet the first is that you never expected Doug to tell me."

He couldn't deny that. Tim Sargent had told him that whatever else Hammond might be, he had a reputation for being bright, and he knew the law. It would be stupid for him to contact Kelly and jeopardize his case. They had overestimated him.

"All right. There's one."

"What's number two?" she asked. Her lips were trembling. He could deal with her anger, but if she started to cry, he couldn't take that.

"The ultrasound."

She stared at him for a moment. "You've lost your mind."

"You joked about it being a religious experience for me, but you weren't far off the mark. When I saw Sammi inside you, and realized how closely her welfare was connected to yours, it was a sobering experience. Then when you got word that Doug had followed through on his custody threat, and you started having contractions, I knew I had to protect you."

"And just how did you do that?"

"I told Tim to filter all information through me."

"Aha." She nodded once, emphatically. "I wondered why I could never get in touch with him." Then she frowned. "That doesn't explain why you kept things from me after she was born. Didn't you think I had the right to know what was going on?"

"It wasn't necessary for you to know every little thing."

"You don't think a court date and the countersuit are more than little things?"

"Of course they're not little. But now they're never going to happen."

"But what if they had? When were you going to tell me if I had to show up? Or were you going to keep that little thing from me while you and Tim handled it? How would that have looked to the judge when Sammi's mother didn't see fit to show up?"

"If it had gotten that far, I would have told you. And I'd have been right there beside you."

"Cut it out, Mike. Don't be charming and sweet and all those other things you do to distract me when I'm mad at you."

"Do you want to hear the rest of my reasons?"

She shook her head. "Just cut to the chase."

"Tim and I worked out a strategy."

"And just what was that?" she asked.

"The counter. It's exactly what I told him. He didn't want Sammi. He wanted the partnership. If we turned up the heat, he had to get out because the bad publicity would cost him everything."

"If you were so sure it would work, why didn't you let me in on it? Why would that have upset me?"

"I was trying to give you some worry-free time with Sammi, to get to know her, enjoy her. I knew Hammond would drop the custody thing and there was no reason for you to go through all the ups and downs of the legal system. Nine times out of ten complaints are settled out of court."

"What if this was the tenth time? What if I'd had to face a judge? Didn't you think I'd need to prepare?"

"That's why you have a lawyer."

"No. You have a lawyer and a friend. I have neither."

Mike winced. "That's ridiculous. I'm your friend."

She was taking this a lot harder than he'd thought. He'd figured protecting her and Sammi was the most important thing. He still thought so.

Kelly wasn't sure whether to slug him or hug him. But when it sank in that he'd broken the cardinal rule of their friendship, she wanted to cry. For as long as she could remember, when she'd had a problem, Mike was always the first person she'd thought of to share it with. He had always talked things over with her, too.

When he'd injured his elbow playing ball, he'd called her right after the doctor broke the news that his career was over. When he'd had the surgery to repair the damage, he'd asked her to be there. When her mother had died, they had gone to each other. She'd comforted him first and found she'd received more consolation than she'd given.

But now she was his wife. And he hadn't seen fit to discuss with her anything about the custody case involving her baby. To protect her, he'd said. He'd never shown that protective streak before, at least not by keeping things from her.

"Friends don't stab each other in the back," she said.

"I was trying to keep you safe from all of it. You had your hands full with a brand-new baby. Every time Sammi sneezed, you worried about her being sick. Half the time you didn't get more than four or five hours of sleep a night. You didn't need to be kept awake by the threat of that jerk taking her away from you. It was never going to happen. I thought the best thing was to spare you the day-to-day ups and downs.''

"I believe you." He was telling the truth. She could see that. Mike couldn't lie any better than she could.

"I'm glad."

"The truth is I blame myself more than you. I went on about how this was my problem and my responsibility to deal with it. I should have demanded that Tim give me more details about what he was doing, or gotten another lawyer. It just never occurred to me that you were in cahoots with him and keeping important details from me.''

Mike was actually being very sweet and considerate. A classic case of the wrong thing for the right reasons. And if the very foundation of their friendship hadn't been open and honest communication, she could probably overlook this slip. But the fact was, she had married Mike against her better judgment. It had been the best decision at the time, and she'd done it for Sammi. But now everything had changed.

Including her. This was the worst possible time to discover this, but it was as clear to her as a freshly spritzed mirror. Even Doug had seen it.

She was in love with Mike.

His eyes narrowed with concern as he studied her. "I only gave you four reasons why I kept it from you. Don't you want to hear the other six?"

"No." She brushed past him. "I'm going upstairs to fold diapers."

"Do you want some help?"

"No, thanks. I'd like to be alone."

"I can give you ten good reasons why you shouldn't—"

"I'll be down when Sammi wakes up," she said over her shoulder.

She wanted to take his ten reasons and stuff them up his nose. There was only one reason why he hadn't talked this over with her.

She *had* lost him.

Or at least she was well on her way to losing him. Because she loved him. The day they had said "I do" was the beginning of the end. Their friendship would never be what it was because of the marriage. Living with Mike had made her see that he was everything she'd ever wanted in a man.

She stopped halfway up the stairs. Living with him? What if she *didn't* live with him? Now that Doug had agreed to sign off his rights to Sammi, she and Mike didn't have to present a united front. They could stick to the original time frame of their agreement. Four months was almost up.

Divorce. Divide and conquer. It was her only chance. If she left, maybe she could still salvage her relationship with Mike. That was the answer, and as far as she could see, her only hope.

Mike turned into the drive. He had just come from Tim Sargent's office and was eager to tell Kelly the news. During the last week, she had kept her distance, a fact that was driving him crazy. He hoped his news would bring them closer, the way they'd been before he'd chosen poorly and tried to protect her. But whatever happened between him and Kelly wouldn't change the decision he'd made today.

He was learning a lot about this loneliness thing. The phrase *lonely in a crowd* sprang to mind. Kelly and

Sammi lived in his house, but they couldn't have been farther apart if she lived in Timbuktu.

It was all his fault, a major error in judgment to keep things from her. He had even told her so. And she knew how much he hated admitting that. It was one step removed from losing. But when he had said it, her response had been, "Doing the wrong thing for the right reasons still makes it wrong."

He couldn't fight her logic. He could only do his best to prove it would never happen again.

At the top of the drive he saw a small, unfamiliar compact car. It looked like Kelly had company. He hoped whoever it was wouldn't stay long. He couldn't wait to talk to Kelly alone.

He burst through the front door and called out, "Kelly? Where are you?"

"In the living room," she said.

He rounded the corner and found Kelly sitting on the couch. At the opposite end, a white-haired woman held Sammi. She was trim and fashionably dressed. The baby seemed comfortable in her arms. As he descended the one step into the room, Kelly and the stranger stared at him.

Kelly sat on the edge of the cushion, her hands clasped in her lap. "Mike, this is Sylvia Fellwock. Sylvia, Mike Cameron."

Her tone was businesslike and steady. There was less warmth than she used to send one of her students to the dean of discipline.

The woman lifted the baby slightly, indicating that she couldn't do the polite thing and shake hands. "How do you do, Mr. Cameron. It's a pleasure to meet you."

"The pleasure's mine," he said. "Call me Mike."

The woman smiled at Sammi and said, "You have a beautiful baby."

"Thanks." He didn't bother correcting her because he thought of Sammi as his daughter. He couldn't love her more if she was his own flesh and blood. "She is beautiful, isn't she? The spitting image of her mother."

Sylvia looked at Kelly, then back at the baby. "Yes, I think you're right."

Mike hunched down beside them and gently stroked Sammi's cheek as he talked to Kelly's friend. "It's nice of you to come by for a visit. I thought I'd met most of Kelly's friends—"

Kelly cleared her throat. "Sylvia answered the ad for child care that I placed in the *Signal*."

His gaze shot to hers. "Child care? You never said anything about that." He didn't want a stranger taking care of Sammi. What could Kelly know about a woman who responded to a newspaper ad? "Why were you looking in the want ads, Sylvia? Have you had children of your own?"

Kelly glared at him. "Mike, I'll handle this."

"That's all right, Mrs. Cameron. I respect your husband for getting involved. So many men let their wives take on the whole burden when they go back to work."

Work? Kelly was going back to work? He hadn't thought about it since they'd first discussed it, when they'd come up with the terms of their agreement. Kelly had insisted on a time limit, because she didn't want him to put his life on hold indefinitely. She had said she was going back in September.

Somehow he thought she would have changed her mind after the baby was born. And that was okay with him. He knew Kelly. He knew it would tear her apart to leave Sammi. Why was she going through with this?

She didn't have to. He would take care of them. Why hadn't she talked it over with him?

Sylvia turned her blue-eyed gaze on Mike. She looked honest and straightforward, but he'd wager Ma Barker had appeared the epitome of maternal perfection when it had suited her.

Sylvia gently bounced the baby when she fussed a little. "I had three children, two boys and a girl. They're grown now. The boys are married, and my daughter is away at college. UCLA."

"Good basketball school, but the football team could use some beefing up."

Sylvia laughed. "That's just what Heather says."

Mike stood and crossed his arms over his chest. "I'd think after raising your family you'd want to take it easy, have time to yourself. Why would you want to tie yourself down with a baby?" He glanced at Kelly and didn't miss the hostile look she shot him.

"I don't need the money, Mr. Cameron. I guess I wanted something to fill my time, something useful. I love children, especially babies." She shrugged. "I suppose I was lonely."

He stared at the baby for a few seconds, then at Kelly. "I can relate to that."

"Why would you be lonely?" Sylvia asked. "You have it all, right here." She let Sammi's tiny fist curl around her finger and smiled as the baby cooed.

"You seem like a nice woman, Sylvia," he said. Even to himself he sounded as sincere as a used-car salesman. "Kelly and I will talk this over and let you know."

Kelly stood up. When he met her gaze, the daggers there made him flinch. "Mike, I know you're trying to help, but I'm handling this just fine."

"If there's nothing else, Mrs. Cameron, I'll be going." Sylvia stood and handed the baby to Mike. He put her up on his shoulder, the way she liked, and breathed in the sweet infant smell of her.

Kelly walked over to the other woman and shook her hand. "I'll check out the references you gave me. You understand that I have several more people to interview."

"Of course. You can't be too careful these days. Children are too precious to take any chances."

Kelly nodded. "I have your number. When I've made a decision, I'll call you, one way or the other."

"Thank you, Mrs. Cameron."

Kelly walked her to the door, and Mike stood with the baby in the living room, waiting. They had a few things to settle.

When she returned, she folded her arms over her chest and glared at him. Her dark eyebrows pulled together as she frowned. "You had no right to take over the way you did. What was that all about?"

"I could ask you the same thing."

She stood in front of him, her green eyes sparkling with anger, and all he could think about was kissing her. Making love to her. He needed a woman, and it was time to let her know the woman he needed was her.

There were some things to get out of the way first.

"Why did you advertise for child care?" He patted Sammi's bottom as she turned her head back and forth on his shoulder, trying to get comfortable.

"I'm going back to work in a couple weeks. I need to find someone to watch the baby." She lifted one eyebrow. "Thanks to you, I probably just lost the most qualified applicant."

"What was so good about Sylvia?" he asked.

"She's warm, experienced, and she doesn't charge an arm and a leg, because she truly doesn't need the money. The best part is that she has her own transportation and will come to my home so I don't have to take Sammi out of her environment."

Mike didn't like the fact that she'd said "my home." What did she mean by that? "I don't understand why she wants the job."

"I suspect she would like to be a grandmother, and her sons are not cooperating. Apparently they married career women who, at the very least, are putting off children."

"As opposed to yourself who's planning to let someone else raise your baby."

"That's not fair, Mike."

He sighed. "I know. It was a cheap shot, and I'm sorry."

"I'd like nothing better than to stay home with her. But I have no choice. I have to work—"

"No, you don't," he said.

"If I don't, how will I put a roof over her head, food in her tummy and clothes on her back? You don't get anything for nothing in life."

Her father's words. "Frank Walker was a wise man. I still miss him," he said.

She nodded. "Me, too. But he was right. And I learned how to take care of myself. I'm grateful to him for that. As long as I live, my child will not want for anything."

"Except for the most important thing."

"What's that?"

"You."

Instead of anger now, her eyes sparkled with unshed tears. "That was low, Cameron."

"I'm not trying to hurt you, Kelly. I'm trying to help."

"Then I'm completely missing the point."

The baby was limp in his arms now, sound asleep. He needed his concentration for this conversation. He needed to be as persuasive and charming as Kelly always accused him of being. He couldn't do that holding the baby.

"I'll explain the point as soon as I put her down."

"I'll do it," she said. There was almost a desperation in her tone and her expression as she held out her arms. She was thinking about the fact that her time with Sammi was no longer unlimited and she wanted to make the most of it. He knew how she felt. His time with both of them was ticking away. He had to figure out how to stop the clock. If she left, he would miss her like crazy.

"I don't mind putting her to bed," he said. "If we hand her off, it'll wake her up."

"All right," she agreed.

"When I come back, there's something I need to ask you."

She nodded, but he could have sworn there was apprehension in her eyes.

After settling the baby in her crib, Mike joined Kelly in the family room.

When he came in, she stopped pacing and turned to him. "All right. Explain to me how reminding me that someone else will have the pleasure of raising my child is a help to me. And don't say you were just being cruel to be kind."

"Don't go back to work. Stay home with her, here, and let me take care of you both."

Her eyes grew wide, and her jaw dropped. He walked over and nudged it closed with the tip of his finger.

She swallowed. "That wasn't part of the agreement."

"So?"

"We decided to stay together four months. Time is almost up. Everything has worked out beautifully," she said, but her lip trembled slightly. She caught it between her teeth, steadied herself, then continued. "I have Sammi and my job, thanks to you."

"Take a maternity leave."

"I don't need a leave. I've been to the doctor for my final checkup and got the go-ahead for—" she looked down at her hands "—well, for going back to work."

"I just meant you should give yourself some time to think this over. Stay here."

"Four months was enough time for me to straighten out my life. There's no reason to keep yours on hold for me any longer, Mike. The last thing I wanted was for this damned agreement to affect our friendship. If we go on like we are, I'm afraid of what will happen to us. I couldn't stand it if—" Her voice caught, and she covered her mouth and turned her back to him.

His life wasn't on hold. For the first time he felt as if he was living it to the fullest. He had purpose and joy and contentment. He realized that without Kelly and Sammi he had no life.

Mike moved behind her and put his hands on her shoulders. She trembled, then tensed. When he tried to pull her back against him, she resisted at first. Finally, she relaxed and he rubbed her arms.

"Do you remember that we also said the four months could be renegotiated?"

"You suggested it. I never agreed."

Mike knew Kelly could be stubborn. But she was carrying it to the extreme. What was going on with her? She was afraid of something. If he didn't find out what, he would lose her. It was time for the direct approach.

He turned her around and held her upper arms. "Kelly, I don't want you to leave when the four months are up."

She blinked. "Why? Sammi and I have put you out long enough."

"Why do you keep assuming the two of you are an imposition? I like having you here."

"I have to go, Mike."

"No, you don't."

"Yes, I do. I resisted marrying you because I was afraid our friendship would be ruined."

"And that hasn't happened."

Her gaze lowered from his eyes to his lips, and he felt her shiver. "Not yet. But if this situation goes on any longer, it could."

"You're wrong. This 'situation' has brought us closer together."

"Don't say that."

"Why not? What are you afraid of?"

"Change, I guess. What we have is perfect, or at least it was. I want things back the way they were. I don't want it to change."

So, she had noticed the shift between them, too. She

had felt the attraction as strongly as he had. But for some reason she was afraid of it.

"It's too late, Kelly. Things between us already have changed. For the better—"

She shook her head. "Don't you see? I have to go back to work. I have to move out as soon as possible. I have to leave before things change more, while there's a chance to get back what we had."

He hated labels, and now he knew why. They were so limiting; they boxed you in and left no place to go. There was only one way he could think of, one sure-fire method to break down her defenses and show her that change was a good thing. Stimulating.

He tightened his grip on her arms and slowly, but firmly, pulled her toward him.

She held back. "What are you doing?"

With one small tug, he had her against him. He wrapped his arms around her, holding her tightly to him. "I'm going to kiss you."

He silenced her protest with his mouth. Angling his head to make his possession of her lips more complete, he moved slowly and seductively, snuffing her resistance.

He knew it had worked when she moaned and went pliant in his arms. She twined her wrists around his neck and leaned into him. Her breasts pressed and burned into his chest, and he wondered why he had thought he was in control. One or two of her feminine moves had about knocked him on his keister. And he didn't mind one little bit.

Things *had* changed for the better between them. Their relationship had gone to a higher plane, and he didn't dare name it. Even though she taught English, Kelly would never admit that she had as much trouble with labels as he did. There was no room for words now. It was time to just feel, and let sensation take them.

Mike trailed kisses over her cheek and traced the curve of her ear with his tongue. He smiled at the ripple that shook her, then groaned when she stood on tiptoe and did the same to him.

"Kelly, I want you. Let me love you—"

She went still in his arms, then leaned her forehead against his chest. Finally she looked up at him and whispered, "Don't say that, Mike."

"I know you want me, too."

"I'd be lying if I denied that. I just can't—" Her eyes pleaded with him to understand.

He didn't and decided to take matters into his own hands, or arms. He scooped her up and started to carry her toward the bedroom.

"What are you doing?" she asked, startled.

"I'm ending our friendship."

"No—"

"So we can move forward—"

"Put me down, Mike. I can't do this."

He stopped instantly and held her for a moment, savoring her softness, her fragile femininity, before letting her slide down the length of him. When he let her go, she put distance between them and stopped in front of the breakfast bar. Her shoulders lifted as she drew a deep breath of air into her lungs.

"Why, Kelly? What's wrong?"

Sadness and confusion twisted together on her face, and he wanted to hold her. All he wanted to do was make her happy. He'd sure screwed that up.

"Mike, will you take care of Sammi for me? For a little while?"

"You know I will. But where are you going?"

"To look for an apartment."

She grabbed her purse and keys. Before she could walk out, he moved in front of her. "Don't do it. Talk to me, Kelly."

She shook her head. "It's too late for that."

"We've always been able to talk. No matter what the problem. Tell me what's wrong."

"As soon as I find a place of my own, everything will be fine again. Please get out of my way, Mike."

Running a hand through his hair, he stepped aside. Short of playing the Neanderthal, he had no way to stop her. When the front door slammed, he gritted his teeth. He couldn't believe she was really going to leave. He didn't want to believe it.

He'd been saying he didn't believe in love for so long, he figured he wouldn't recognize it if it reached out and bit him in the butt. Which was exactly what had happened. Hell of a time to figure it out, at the same moment the windows stopped rattling from her slamming the door as she left. The fact was, he loved her.

He had done everything but come out and tell her how he felt. Why was she running away from it? Was she still holding out for Prince Charming?

"I'm not the tights and cape type." He stared at the front door as silence echoed through the house. "But I love you, Kel."

Chapter Eleven

Kelly drove around Newhall for a while but couldn't bring herself to stop at any apartment buildings with For Rent signs in front. She was so confused. She needed someone to talk to. She needed her best friend. She needed Mike. But she couldn't talk to him about him, so she settled for Susan.

When she pulled up in front of the Wisharts', two young men were shooting hoops in the driveway. Kelly had met Brian and Scott once before. She smiled, remembering Susan saying that she had been tempted to call them Don Juan and Lothario. The names would have been appropriate. They were darn cute.

"Hi, guys," she said, walking past them on the concrete driveway to the front door. "Is your mom home?"

Brian, the oldest at twenty, caught and held the basketball. He was tall and blond and lanky. "She's at the grocery store. Should be back soon, though, if you'd like to wait."

"Thanks. I need to talk to her about something."

"Want to play a little one-on-one?" Scott grinned at her. He was about the same height as his brother, good-looking and blond. He seemed to be a fun-loving eighteen-year-old who, from all reports, had been a Casanova since a girl had put that first note in his kindergarten cubby. Kelly could see why. He was an outrageous flirt.

She smiled, responding to his charm. "Sure. You don't think I can play, do you?"

"Show me." He tossed her the ball, and she caught it easily. His eyebrows went up in surprise.

She bounced it a couple times, then moved toward the hoop and pushed the ball off her palm. It missed. "I'm a little rusty. I just had a baby, you know."

"Yeah. We heard," Brian said. "Mom said she's real cute."

"I think so. Mike says—"

"How is Coach?" Scott asked. "He was so cool when I played football last year."

"He's fine." Kelly bounced the ball a couple times. She looked at the guys and before she could stop it, the question popped out. "I'd like to ask you something. Do you think a man and a woman can have a fulfilling platonic friendship?"

Scott's blue eyes widened as he looked at his brother. "Bro, you want to field that one?"

"You've had all the experience," Brian said, his lean cheeks suspiciously pink. "You tell her."

Susan's husband, Brad, opened the front door. Both boys turned and spoke at the same time. "Hi, Dad."

Brad's eyebrows lifted in surprise. "I haven't had a greeting that enthusiastic since you were little and I came home from a business trip with presents. If I didn't know better, I'd say you were glad to see me.''

"We're always glad to see you, oh ancient wise man," Scott said. "You're just in time. Kelly has a question for you."

"Hi, Kelly." Brad sent her a friendly smile. "Nice to see you."

"Hi, Brad," she answered.

The boys started shooting baskets again as she joined their father on the front porch. She looked down at the welcome mat, and she smiled wryly at the words, Wipe Your Feet, Stupid. Leave it to an English teacher. An appropriate saying with a healthy dose of self-esteem thrown in.

"What's the question?" Brad asked.

"Can a man and a woman have a satisfying platonic friendship without getting physical? I need a man's point of view. You're a man."

"That wasn't exactly a question, but I can answer with a reasonable amount of certainty. I am a man."

"Can things stay the same? I mean, why complicate a perfectly functional friendship with man-woman stuff?"

When he stroked his beard, she knew she had come to the right place to talk. He looked the essence of wisdom, in spite of the mismatched plaid shorts and striped shirt. After all, wise men weren't expected to be snappy dressers. Take Doug, for instance. Always looked like a fashion plate, and he'd turned out to be a jerk and just another pretty face.

But then there was Mike. Good dresser, good-looking. Good God, she was so muddled.

Brad stared at the ground for a while. Then he stuck his hands in his shorts pockets. "That's a good question. I think it probably depends on the man and woman involved." At the sound of a car, he glanced up. "Look here. Susan's back," he said, a distinct note of relief in his voice.

The garage door went up, stopping the basketball game, and Susan drove into the garage. As automatic as the door, Brad and the boys opened the rear of the compact station wagon and disappeared into the house with groceries.

Susan joined Kelly on the front porch. "Hi. What's wrong?"

"What makes you think there's something wrong?"

"I know my men. Unloading the car usually takes an act of Congress around here. They did it without being asked, including my cute but unobservant husband. For him it takes a nuclear explosion to blast him loose from the couch."

"Are you saying I've cleared the room?"

"Yeah."

Kelly was surprised. She'd thought her question had been cloaked in idle conversation and veiled in humor. She followed Susan into the house. In the kitchen, plastic bags of groceries littered the circular oak table, tile countertops and the floor. Susan rifled them, pulling things out and putting them away. As Kelly emptied the one closest to her on the table, she marveled at the amount of food it took to feed a family of four, two of which were young men. It made her glad she'd had a girl. Especially since she would be single soon and on her own with Sammi.

"Susan?" The other woman turned and met her gaze. "I'm leaving Mike."

Shock widened Susan's eyes. "Why? What did he do?"

"Nothing. It's me—"

"He must have done something. Although I can't imagine what. He's really a sweetie."

"All he did was try to change the rules."

Susan slanted her a sardonic look. "Good God, how could he? The man should be drawn and quartered."

"Be serious."

"All right. I have a feeling there's something I don't know. You want to fill in the blanks?"

Kelly nodded. If she was going to get good advice, Susan needed the facts. "Mike married me to save my job, give my baby a name and help me keep custody of my baby if Doug sued me."

"So Mike's not the father?"

"You believed that rumor?"

"It wouldn't have surprised me. Like I said at the wedding, a blind man could see that there's something special between the two of you." Susan looked at her as she wadded up a plastic bag. "So did Doug sue?"

Kelly nodded. "Mike steered me to a lawyer friend of his, then proceeded to keep me in the dark about what was going on. To protect me he said."

"You sound upset about that."

"I am. Mike and I have always talked to each other about everything. He shut me out of this. I don't know if I can get over that."

"Like I said, draw and quarter Sir Walter Raleigh for being your hero. He's got it coming if you ask me."

Kelly was starting to get irritated. This was not the sort of satisfaction she'd expected from Susan. "That's what I meant about changing the rules. We had an agreement to stay married four months. Just before school starts, I was supposed to move out. I could be a divorced single mother and keep my job, just not a single mother, never been married.''

''So what's the problem?''

''Mike wants me to stay.''

Susan gasped in mock horror. ''How awful!''

Kelly glared at her. ''Whose side are you on, anyhow?''

''The side of true love.''

''Two four-letter words back-to-back,'' Kelly muttered in disgust. ''Cameron would eat that up.''

''What?'' Susan opened a brand new package of chocolate-covered caramel cookies and held it out.

''Nothing.'' Kelly took one and bit into it. ''Speaking of the L-word,'' she said, ''I think he loves me.''

Susan's gaze snapped to hers so fast, Kelly was surprised she didn't have whiplash. ''He said that?''

''No, but I'd bet anything that he wants to,'' Kelly said sadly.

''Rip the man's tongue out.''

''Come on, Suse. You're supposed to be helping.''

''How do you feel about him?''

''I love him.''

Susan brushed a strand of blond hair from her forehead. A puzzled expression wrinkled her brow. ''I don't get it. If you're in love with him and he's crazy about you, why are you leaving him?''

''I can't believe you don't understand.''

''And I can't believe you're discussing this with me. Mike's the one you should be talking to.''

That was the first thing Susan had said that made sense to her. Now she knew why she'd come here. Every once in a while she needed a good mental slap. She'd just gotten it. She consulted Mike about everything else. It had gotten to be a habit, one she didn't want to break.

She walked over to her friend and took another cookie. Then she hugged the other woman. "I was wrong. You should never teach biology," she said.

Susan grinned. "I don't plan to. I've got my lesson plans under control."

"With a name like Wishart I'm surprised you don't give better advice in the man-woman department."

Susan took her by the shoulders, turned her and gave her a gentle nudge toward the door. "Here's some advice. Go be loquacious with that hunky husband of yours."

Chapter Twelve

"Susan says I have to talk to you, Mike." Kelly stood in the master bedroom, watching him towel dry his dark, wet hair.

"I wanted to talk, and you ran out of here like a wide receiver looking to break a record," he said, staring at her. "But Susan tells you to do it, and it's okay?"

"I'm confused. Please don't make this harder." Kelly set her purse and keys on the dresser. "Is Sammi all right?"

"Fine. She's been fed, bathed and is now taking her afternoon nap." He draped the towel over his shoulder and crossed his arms over his bare chest. "What else did Susan say?"

"Nothing."

He shook his head. "Work with me, Kel. If she didn't say anything, how did she change your mind about talking?"

"She said you should be drawn and quartered and have your tongue ripped out."

"Good God, what did I ever do to her?"

"Nothing. It was tongue-in-cheek humor." A small smile pulled at her lips for a moment. It had seemed easy when she'd been with Susan. Now that she was facing her hunky husband, *loquacious* was the last thing she wanted to be. *Folded in his strong arms* was the first thing that came to mind. *Kissed* was number two on the list. None of the above came under the heading of friendship.

"I'm glad she was kidding. But she must have said something right. You're here."

"I have this problem, Mike."

"What is it? Maybe I can help."

"I've got this problem with a friend. I need to talk to you about it."

"Susan couldn't help you with it?"

She lifted one shoulder. "I've never been able to confide in anyone the way I can in you."

"I see." One corner of his mouth lifted in that half grin that made her heart race and her pulse pound.

"You're not going to make this easy, are you?" she asked.

"Should I?"

"I'll give you ten good reasons why you should."

Her eyes dropped to the towel knotted around his middle. If things went in a certain direction, this could be the second time she saw him naked.

"Why should I make this easy for you?" he asked.

"Because you're the last of the really nice guys. And you'd be doing it for you, me, Sammi, Susan, Brad, their children, my brother—"

"Wait a minute. I'll go along with you, me and Sammi, but you're cheating with the rest."

"No. I'll drive them nuts if you don't make this easy on me and listen."

"So talk. I'm all ears. Tell me about this problem with your friend. Is this person male or female?"

"Male."

A glow crept into his dark gaze that set off a wildfire in the pit of her belly. "Do I know him?"

She nodded. "He's the best friend I've ever had."

"So what's this problem you've got with him?"

"He doesn't want to be friends anymore."

"What does he want?"

"A wife." She looked at him. "That four-letter word about sums it up."

"Why does it scare you that things are changing? There's nothing wrong with starting out as friends and taking it from there."

She wasn't so sure about that. "What we had was a perfect friendship. It worked—" she hesitated, searching for the right adjective "—perfectly."

"What makes you think it won't work if you become a wife to him?"

"He was married once."

"And you think he doesn't want to be married again?"

"No, he made it clear that he does. And that's the problem."

"It's obvious I'm the friend, Kelly. I do want to be married to you. If you have a problem with that, I need you to spell it out." He rubbed the back of his neck. "I'm not the brightest guy in the world."

"Why do you do that? Put yourself down that way? You're one of the smartest people I know."

"I've been alone too long. I'm not very good at this relationship stuff. I'm selfish and—"

"How can you say that? You've taken me into your home, married me to save my job and my baby. That's pretty unselfish if you ask me."

"I'm not perfect, you know. I'm opinionated and think I know what's best. I don't mean to, but I tend to bulldoze people."

"But everyone who really knows you understands that you wouldn't intentionally hurt anyone. Your heart's in the right place."

"Speaking of hearts, I didn't mean to scare you off before. When I said I was ending our friendship, you didn't let me finish. It's not over, just…heating up."

Her pulse raced. "What are you saying, Mike?"

"I know you're holding out for romantic love. God knows I'm not the most romantic guy in the world. But I do love you, Kel."

"I was afraid of that." She turned away, toward the mirror on the dresser. It was a useless gesture in shutting him out since he was right behind her and she could see his reflection. There was such an earnest look on his face, she had no doubt that he meant what he said.

"I think you love me, too."

"Oh, God…"

"What's wrong with being in love? Lots of people would lie, cheat, beg or steal to find what we have."

"It's catastrophic for us. If I let myself love you, I'll lose you."

He shook his head. "You're gonna have to explain that. I just don't get it."

"I watched your marriage go from love to disaster

to divorce. You never spoke to Carol after that. You never even talked about her."

"Because there was nothing to say."

"You've never lied to me before, Cameron. Don't start now. You talked to me about everything. But you never discussed the divorce. I know it was because it hurt too much to even share it with me."

He made a cross over his heart and held his hand up, palm out. "I swear. I didn't talk about it because there was nothing to say. Carol left me because the days in the spotlight were over. I wanted to work with kids, she wanted the limelight. Afterward, I realized not only that I never loved her, but that I didn't much like her or miss her."

Her gaze raised to his in the mirror. "You're telling me the truth?"

He nodded. Moving one step forward, he put his hands on her arms. After turning her, he cupped her cheek in his palm. "I love you, Kelly Cameron. Not because I feel I owe your family anything, not because I'm a nice guy, not because of the baby. I love you because you're you. I think I've always loved you."

"I love you, Mike. I think I always have, too." Tears of happiness burned her eyes. "By the way, that was eloquent."

"I'm sorry. I know you want romance—"

She silenced him with her finger on his lips. When he drew it into his mouth and sucked, her stomach knotted with need. "I wasn't being critical. That really was eloquent in its simple sincerity." She closed her eyes for a moment and took a deep breath as he kissed her palm. "And in the romance department you could give lessons," she said, her voice growing husky.

"Even after Le Chêne?"

Her eyebrows shot up in surprise. "That was an attempt to sweep me off my feet?"

"It was." The sheepish expression on his face was so endearing it made her want to cry.

She punched him playfully. "I knew you were up to something."

"And you saw how well it worked out."

"Better than you know. I was dined and charmed and so confused, bewildered and amazed by you."

"And afraid that love would destroy the perfect friendship."

"But that's another thing you coached me on." She trailed a finger down his chest and smiled when he sucked in a breath and his dark gaze intensified. "I can have it all. A hunky husband, romantic lover, friend and father all rolled into one nice, neat package."

"And I got a beautiful, sweet, worrywart wife who needs to relax and not talk so much." He lowered his mouth to hers, kissing her deeply. Kelly slid her hands up his chest and looped them around his neck. She was just giving herself up to the magic when he pulled back.

"What is it, Mike?"

"You make me forget everything. I had something to talk to you about earlier, but I lost it when I thought I'd lost you."

"Talk to me quick, Coach." She kissed him lightly on the lips. "If I know our daughter, she'll sleep soundly and long enough for us to—" She raised one eyebrow suggestively.

"Speaking of Sammi, how would you feel about me adopting her?"

"You're already her father in every way."

"I want it to be legal," he said. "I spoke to Tim

about it, just to see if there would be any problems. He said Hammond signed off his rights and nothing would stand in the way of me adopting her. Unless you object—"

She started to cry.

"What's wrong, Kel? It's okay if you don't want me to."

She shook her head as she wiped the tears from her cheeks. "There's nothing I want more. Like I said, you showed me I can have it all—husband, lover, friend, father, all rolled into one."

He grinned. "Then everything's settled."

She glanced at the bed. "Not quite. There's the matter of the lover part—"

"Ah," he said, following her gaze. "I once said you'd be the first to know if I needed a woman."

"You did."

"I need *you*, Kel," he said, meeting her gaze with his own dark one. "I will always need you."

"I need you, too. I love you, Mike Cameron."

He walked to the bed and swept the covers down. Then he walked back to her and lifted her into his arms. The sweet romantic gesture brought a lump to her throat. He carried her to the bed and set her down gently on the sheets, then joined her. With their bodies they signed an agreement more binding than their wedding vows. It was a promise of the heart, a pledge of the soul.

Kelly knew she and her coach would be friends and lovers, husband and wife. It was a good time to swear back on men. At least one man in particular. He was a good one, in fact the best.

*   *   *   *   *

Silhouette's newest series

YOURS TRULY

Love when you least expect it.

Where the written word plays a vital role in uniting
couples—you're guaranteed a fun and exciting read
every time!

Look for Marie Ferrarella's upcoming Yours Truly,
Traci on the Spot, in March 1997.

Here's a special sneak preview....

1

Morgan Brigham slowly set down his coffee cup on the kitchen table and stared at the comic strip in the center of his paper. It was nestled in among approximately twenty others that were spread out across two pages. But this was the only one he made a point of reading faithfully each morning at breakfast.

This was the only one that mirrored *her* life.

He read each panel twice, as if he couldn't trust his own eyes. But he could. It was there, in black and white.

Morgan folded the paper slowly, thoughtfully, his mind not on his task. So Traci was getting engaged.

The realization gnawed at the lining of his stomach. He hadn't a clue as to why.

He had even less of a clue why he did what he did next.

Abandoning his coffee, now cool, and the newspaper, and ignoring the fact that this was going to make him late for the office, Morgan went to get a sheet of stationery from the den.

He didn't have much time.

* * *

Traci Richardson stared at the last frame she had just drawn. Debating, she glanced at the creature sprawled out on the kitchen floor.

"What do you think, Jeremiah? Too blunt?"

The dog, part bloodhound, part mutt, idly looked up from his rawhide bone at the sound of his name. Jeremiah gave her a look she felt free to interpret as ambivalent.

"Fine help you are. What if Daniel actually reads this and puts two and two together?"

Not that there was all that much chance that the man who had proposed to her, the very prosperous and busy Dr. Daniel Thane, would actually see the comic strip she drew for a living. Not unless the strip was taped to a bicuspid he was examining. Lately Daniel had gotten so busy he'd stopped reading anything but the morning headlines of the *Times*.

Still, you never knew. "I don't want to hurt his feelings," Traci continued, using Jeremiah as a sounding board. "It's just that Traci is overwhelmed by Donald's proposal and, see, she thinks the ring is going to swallow her up." To prove her point, Traci held up the drawing for the dog to view.

This time, he didn't even bother to lift his head.

Traci stared moodily at the small velvet box on the kitchen counter. It had sat there since Daniel had asked her to marry him last Sunday. Even if Daniel never read her comic strip, he was going to suspect something eventually. The very fact that she hadn't grabbed the ring from his hand and slid it onto her finger should have told him that she had doubts about their union.

Traci sighed. Daniel was a catch by any definition. So what was her problem? She kept waiting to be struck by that sunny ray of happiness. Daniel said he wanted to take care of her, to fulfill her every wish. And he was even willing to let her think about it before she gave him her answer.

Guilt nibbled at her. She should be dancing up and down, not wavering like a weather vane in a gale.

Pronouncing the strip completed, she scribbled her signature in the corner of the last frame and then sighed. Another week's work put to bed. She glanced at the pile of mail on the counter. She'd been bringing it in steadily from the mailbox since Monday, but the stack had gotten no farther than her kitchen. Sorting letters seemed the least heinous of all the annoying chores that faced her.

Traci paused as she noted a long envelope. Morgan Brigham. Why would Morgan be writing to her?

Curious, she tore open the envelope and quickly scanned the short note inside.

Dear Traci,
I'm putting the summerhouse up for sale. Thought you might want to come up and see it one more time before it goes up on the block. Or make a bid for it yourself. If memory serves, you once said you wanted to buy it. Either way, let me know. My number's on the card.

> Take care,
> Morgan

P.S. Got a kick out of *Traci on the Spot* this week.

Traci folded the letter. He read her strip. She hadn't known that. A feeling of pride silently coaxed a smile to her lips. After a beat, though, the rest of his note seeped into her consciousness. He was selling the house.

The summerhouse. A faded white building with brick trim. Suddenly, memories flooded her mind. Long, lazy afternoons that felt as if they would never end.

Morgan.

She looked at the far wall in the family room. There was a large framed photograph of her and Morgan standing before the summerhouse. Traci and Morgan. Morgan and Traci. Back then, it seemed their lives had been permanently intertwined. A bittersweet feeling of loss passed over her.

Traci quickly pulled the telephone over to her on the counter and tapped out the number on the keypad.

*   *   *   *   *

Look for TRACI ON THE SPOT
by Marie Ferrarella, coming to
Silhouette YOURS TRULY
in March 1997.

Silhouette
ROMANCE™

COMING NEXT MONTH

#1210 MYSTERY MAN—Diana Palmer
Our 50th Fabulous Father!
Fabulous Father Canton Rourke was in Cancun, Mexico, to relax
with his preteen daughter, but damsel-in-distress Janie Curtis was
putting an end to that mission. The perky mystery writer was looking
for a hero able to steal hearts—would Canton prove the perfect
suspect?

#1211 MISS MAXWELL BECOMES A MOM
—Donna Clayton
The Single Daddy Club
Confirmed bachelor Derrick Cheney knew nothing about raising his
young godson—but the boy's teacher, pretty Anna Maxwell, was the
perfect person to give him daddy lessons. Problem was, she was also
giving Derrick ideas to make Miss Maxwell a mom...and his wife.

#1212 MISSING: ONE BRIDE—Alice Sharpe
Surprise Brides
Stop that bride! When groom-to-be Thorn Powell went to track
down his runaway fiancée, maid of honor Alexandra Williams
reluctantly came along. But as the marriage chase went on, Thorn
began wondering if his true bride might be the one riding right beside
him....

#1213 REAL MARRIAGE MATERIAL—Jodi O'Donnell
Turning Jeb Albright into a "respectable gentleman" would
definitely be a challenge for Southern belle Mariah Duncan.
Especially when this strong, rugged Texan had the lovely Mariah
thinking he was real marriage material...just the way he was!

#1214 HUSBAND AND WIFE...AGAIN—Robin Wells
Love and marriage? Divorcée Jamie Erickson had once believed in
the power of both. Then Stone Johnson, her handsome ex-husband,
returned, reawakening memories of the happiness they'd shared, and
setting Jamie to wonder if they could be husband and wife...again!

#1215 DADDY FOR HIRE—Joey Light
Jack was glad to help out single mom Abagail with her children. His
little girl needed a mommy figure as much as her sons needed a male
influence. But Jack soon realized he didn't want to be just a daddy
for hire; he wanted the job forever—with Abagail as his wife!

MILLION DOLLAR SWEEPSTAKES
OFFICIAL RULES
NO PURCHASE NECESSARY TO ENTER

1. To enter, follow the directions published. Method of entry may vary. For eligibility, entries must be received no later than March 31, 1998. No liability is assumed for printing errors, lost, late, non-delivered or misdirected entries.

   To determine winners, the sweepstakes numbers assigned to submitted entries will be compared against a list of randomly, preselected prize winning numbers. In the event all prizes are not claimed via the return of prize winning numbers, random drawings will be held from among all other entries received to award unclaimed prizes.

2. Prize winners will be determined no later than June 30, 1998. Selection of winning numbers and random drawings are under the supervision of D. L. Blair, Inc., an independent judging organization whose decisions are final. Limit: one prize to a family or organization. No substitution will be made for any prize, except as offered. Taxes and duties on all prizes are the sole responsibility of winners. Winners will be notified by mail. Odds of winning are determined by the number of eligible entries distributed and received.

3. Sweepstakes open to residents of the U.S. (except Puerto Rico), Canada and Europe who are 18 years of age or older, except employees and immediate family members of Torstar Corp., D. L. Blair, Inc., their affiliates, subsidiaries, and all other agencies, entities, and persons connected with the use, marketing or conduct of this sweepstakes. All applicable laws and regulations apply. Sweepstakes offer void wherever prohibited by law. Any litigation within the province of Quebec respecting the conduct and awarding of a prize in this sweepstakes must be submitted to the Régie des alcools, des courses et des jeux. In order to win a prize, residents of Canada will be required to correctly answer a time-limited arithmetical skill-testing question to be administered by mail.

4. Winners of major prizes (Grand through Fourth) will be obligated to sign and return an Affidavit of Eligibility and Release of Liability within 30 days of notification. In the event of non-compliance within this time period or if a prize is returned as undeliverable, D. L. Blair, Inc. may at its sole discretion, award that prize to an alternate winner. By acceptance of their prize, winners consent to use of their names, photographs or other likeness for purposes of advertising, trade and promotion on behalf of Torstar Corp., its affiliates and subsidiaries, without further compensation unless prohibited by law. Torstar Corp. and D. L. Blair, Inc., their affiliates and subsidiaries are not responsible for errors in printing of sweepstakes and prize winning numbers. In the event a duplication of a prize winning number occurs, a random drawing will be held from among all entries received with that prize winning number to award that prize.

5. This sweepstakes is presented by Torstar Corp., its subsidiaries and affiliates in conjunction with book, merchandise and/or product offerings. The number of prizes to be awarded and their value are as follows: Grand Prize — $1,000,000 (payable at $33,333.33 a year for 30 years); First Prize — $50,000; Second Prize — $10,000; Third Prize — $5,000; 3 Fourth Prizes — $1,000 each; 10 Fifth Prizes — $250 each; 1,000 Sixth Prizes — $10 each. Values of all prizes are in U.S. currency. Prizes in each level will be presented in different creative executions, including various currencies, vehicles, merchandise and travel. Any presentation of a prize level in a currency other than U.S. currency represents an approximate equivalent to the U.S. currency prize for that level, at that time. Prize winners will have the opportunity of selecting any prize offered for that level; however, the actual non U.S. currency equivalent prize if offered and selected, shall be awarded at the exchange rate existing at 3:00 P.M. New York time on March 31, 1998. A travel prize option, if offered and selected by winner, must be completed within 12 months of selection and is subject to: traveling companion(s) completing and returning of a Release of Liability prior to travel; and hotel and flight accommodations availability. For a current list of all prize options offered within prize levels, send a self-addressed, stamped envelope (WA residents need not affix postage) to: MILLION DOLLAR SWEEPSTAKES Prize Options, P.O. Box 4456, Blair, NE 68009-4456, USA.

6. For a list of prize winners (available after July 31, 1998) send a separate, stamped, self-addressed envelope to: MILLION DOLLAR SWEEPSTAKES Winners, P.O. Box 4459, Blair, NE 68009-4459, USA.

As seen on TV!
Free Gift Offer

With a Free Gift proof-of-purchase from any Silhouette® book,
you can receive a beautiful cubic zirconia pendant.

This gorgeous marquise-shaped stone is a genuine cubic
zirconia—accented by an 18" gold tone necklace.
(Approximate retail value $19.95)

Send for yours today...
compliments of  *Silhouette*®

To receive your free gift, a cubic zirconia pendant, send us one original proof-of-purchase, photocopies not accepted, from the back of any Silhouette Romance™, Silhouette Desire®, Silhouette Special Edition®, Silhouette Intimate Moments® or Silhouette Yours Truly™ title available in February, March and April at your favorite retail outlet, together with the Free Gift Certificate, plus a check or money order for $1.65 U.S./$2.15 CAN. (do not send cash) to cover postage and handling, payable to Silhouette Free Gift Offer. We will send you the specified gift. Allow 6 to 8 weeks for delivery. Offer good until April 30, 1997 or while quantities last. Offer valid in the U.S. and Canada only.

Free Gift Certificate

Name: _____

Address: _____

City: _____ State/Province: _____ Zip/Postal Code: _____

Mail this certificate, one proof-of-purchase and a check or money order for postage and handling to: SILHOUETTE FREE GIFT OFFER 1997. In the U.S.: 3010 Walden Avenue, P.O. Box 9077, Buffalo NY 14269-9077. In Canada: P.O. Box 613, Fort Erie, Ontario L2Z 5X3.

FREE GIFT OFFER   084-KFD
ONE PROOF-OF-PURCHASE
To collect your fabulous FREE GIFT, a cubic zirconia pendant, you must include this
original proof-of-purchase for each gift with the properly completed Free Gift Certificate.

084-KFD

twins
on the doorstep
by Stella Bagwell

When the Murdock sisters found abandoned twins
on their ranch-house doorstep, they had no clue the
little ones would lead them to love!

Come see how each sister meets her match—and how
the twins' family is discovered—in

THE SHERIFF'S SON (SR #1218, April 1997)

THE RANCHER'S BRIDE (SR #1224, May 1997)

THE TYCOON'S TOTS (SR #1228, June 1997)

TWINS ON THE DOORSTEP—a brand-new miniseries
by Stella Bagwell starting in April...
Only from

Silhouette ROMANCE™

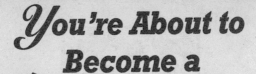